SEIZING A GANGSTA'S HEART FOR THE SUMMER

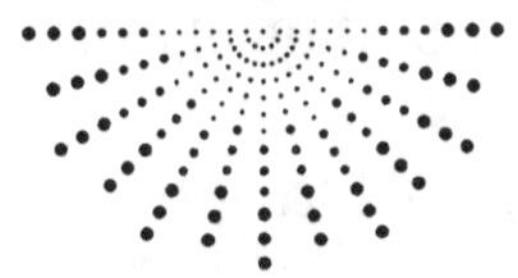

NAI

URBAN AINT DEAD

Email: urbanaintdead@gmail.com

ISBN: 979-8-9904701-9-4

STAY UP TO DATE

To stay up to date on new releases, plus get information on
contests, sneak peaks and more,
Click the link below...
https://mailchi.mp/6d21003686d1/subscribe

CONTENTS

<u>**Soundtracks**</u>

Scan the QR Code below to listen to the Soundtracks/Singles of some of your favorite U.A.D titles:

Don't have Spotify or Apple Music?
No Sweat!
Visit your choice streaming platform and search URBAN AINT DEAD.

Currently on lock serving a bid?
JPay, iHeartRadio, WHATEVER!
We got you covered.

Simply log into your facility's kiosk or tablet, go to music and search URBAN AINT DEAD.

URBAN AINT DEAD

Like & Follow us on social media:
FB - URBAN AINT DEAD
IG: @urbanaintdead
Tik Tok - @urbanaintdead

<u>**Submissions**</u>

Submit the first three chapters of your completed manuscript to <u>urbanaintdead@gmail.com</u>, subject line: Your book's title. The manuscript must be in a .doc file and sent as an attachment. The document should be in Times New Roman, double-spaced, and in size 12 font. Also, provide your synopsis and full contact information. If sending multiple submissions, they must each be in a separate email. Have a story but no way to submit it electronically? You can still submit to URBAN AINT DEAD. Send in the first three chapters, written or typed, of your completed manuscript to:

URBAN AINT DEAD
P.O Box 448
Maybrook, NY 12543

DO NOT send original manuscript. Must be a duplicate.
Provide your synopsis and a cover letter containing your full contact information.
Thanks for considering URBAN AINT DEAD.

1

ALACEA

I pushed my G-Wagon to its limit on the way home to my condo that I sometimes shared with my lover, Quan. It was a little past one in the morning, and I'd ditched another girls' night to go lay up with Mr. For Everybody. A small part of me was ashamed to say that I'd been waiting on his text since the moment I stepped out tonight. While I loved a good turn up just as much as the next person, if I had to choose, I would much rather be laid up with my man. My friends were over me, and sometimes I felt the same, but that didn't stop me from dropping everything to be up under him.

My relationship with Quan was so complicated, a little toxic, yet so intensely wrapped in love. I couldn't fully put together words to describe who we were to each other. What couldn't be disputed was that I was completely enthralled with the six-foot tall, slender built, caramel skin colored man with lying eyes. NayQuan Prince Stokes was the shit to me. I knew he was bad for my heart, but in some ways, he was good to my soul.

It was crazy that the same person that caused me heartache was the only one who could put my heart back together. Pulling my truck into the building's parking garage, I parked in my assigned spot next to his but didn't see his car. I thought nothing of it because as lazy as Quan was, I could count on him to Uber every now and then to get out of driving. Taking my keys out of the ignition, I went to step out and heard my phone ring. By the ringtone, I knew it was my cousin, Ashlynn, calling. I knew she felt a way about me leaving the lounge early, but she wouldn't let the night go by without making sure I made it home safely.

"**Hello,**" I answered, hitting the lock button on my key fob and continuing on to the elevator.

"**You made it in?**"

"**Just parked. Headed upstairs now.**"

"**Okay, cool. Love you. Night.**"

"**Ash, really?**" I knew she was rushing me off the phone because she was mad, but it wasn't that serious.

"**Really what? I called to make sure you got home. I don't have nothing else to say but good night, Lacey.**"

Sucking my teeth, I sighed. "**Okay. I'ma give you a call tomorrow.**"

"**I'm gonna be out most of the day, so I'll give you a call**

when I'm free." She was dismissive in her tone, and I didn't appreciate it at all.

"You know what, Ash? I understand how you feel about my relationship, but it's really not that serious." In the elevator, I pressed my floor and folded my arms tightly, annoyed that she was doing the most.

"You know what? Since you won't let me leave this phone call gracefully, I'ma just go head and get this off my chest. It's very serious to me when I see you almost trippin' over your own feet to go see bout a nigga who you couldn't even get to answer your texts earlier. I've watched you let that nigga play in yo face the last two years, and most of the time, I've held my tongue. But that shit burns me up how you've let that relationship not only change you but define you. Please stop me when I'm lying."

I let her words sink in as they hit me in the chest. Ashlynn wasn't just my cousin; she was my confidant. We always told each other the real. It just so happened that I had been on the receiving end of those talks since I'd been with Quan. And though most of the time I didn't want to hear it, I knew I needed it.

"I hear you, Ash. Still, I can't help who I love."

"I know that, Lacey. You can't help who you love, but you can help what you allow. I love you, cousin. Good night." She ended the call before I could say anything else.

Conflicted and wanting to be held, I waited impatiently for the elevator to reach my floor. When it dinged, I already had my keys out. As I went to stick the key in the door, my phone rang again. This time, it was Quan calling. I picked up before the phone could ring a second time.

"Hey, baby. You must've heard me outside the door. I was just about to turn my key."

"Damn, bae. I thought I'd be able to catch you before you made it home." His background was silent, and I assumed it was because he was inside waiting on me.

"Why? You wanted me to pick you up some food, huh, greedy?" Unlocking the door, I entered my place. The house was pitch black, making my mood instantly switch because I knew why.

"Nah, bae. I had some..."

"Business to take care of." I cut him off and finished his infamous excuse.

"Yeah. And I'm sorry bout this. It was some last-minute shit I had to handle."

Closing the door behind me, I kicked my heels off and navigated the darkness until I reached the living room.

"I was hoping you wouldn't do this shit to me tonight. You are so fuckin' inconsiderate, NayQuan. You knew I was out with Ash and them when you called. Why would you wait for me to ditch them and get all the way home to say some shit? Like come on." Throwing my purse on the couch, I plopped down next to it.

"Fuck all dat. You ain't need to be out when you got a man at home."

"You sound crazy as hell. What man, nigga?!" I yelled

out, pissed. **"Unless you bout to pop out of a closet some-where in here, then I don't have a man at home."**

"Ay, man, you want a nigga wit some shit going on, or you want a bum?"

I rolled my eyes so far up in the air that I was surprised they didn't get stuck. **"Cut the bullshit, okay? It's almost two in the fuckin' morning, and the reason you're not here don't have shit to do with no money. And I ain't never known you to work nobody corner so miss me. Ain't shit needing your attention right now but a bitch. The least you can do is be honest with me. For once, give me that courtesy."** I felt myself about to cry and threw my head back to stop the tears from falling.

The phone got quiet on his end, confirming what I already knew to be true. The love I had for Quan allowed me to ignore his doggish ways, choosing to only focus on the good aspects of the relationship. And that was where I fucked up at.

"Alacea, a nigga ain't on that typa time. I really had to bust a move. I was on my way over there when I got the call."

"I'ma go because I know my mouth, and if I stay on this phone any longer, shit gon' go left. Bye, Quan." I wanted to hang up but held the line open, hoping he'd say something that would convince me that he wasn't on bullshit.

"I'ma hit you first thing in the morning, bae. I prom-ise." Shaking my head, I went to hang up when I heard the distinct sound of a baby crying.

"Whose ba…"

"Love you, bae. Hit you tomorrow."

The call ended abruptly, and I had a nagging feeling that made my stomach turn.

You can't help who you love, but you can help what you allow. Ashlynn's words rang loud and clear in my head. Those tears that I'd forced myself not to shed came trickling down my face. I was vulnerable to this love. I knew it, and Quan knew it. With nothing left to do, I set my phone to DND and stripped out of my clothes. Not bothering to go to my bedroom, I pulled my throw blanket over my body and forced my eyes closed.

Before I could get comfortable enough to fall into a not so peaceful slumber, I could hear my business phone ring in my purse. I really didn't feel like dealing with anyone tonight, but if someone was calling, it was an emergency. It was always an emergency. Pulling the blanket off of me, I sat up to retrieve the phone, only for the ringing to stop and start back up almost immediately. Seeing my brother's name on the screen, I answered.

"Yeah?"

"Why you didn't answer when I first called, Lacey?" His stern voice came through, making me roll my eyes. Ten years my senior, he acted more like my father than my brother.

"Cause I was drifting off to sleep, Lance. I just got in a few minutes ago."

"Oh. Are you up for service?"

"Depends on what it is. I had a couple drinks, and I

don't wanna take on nothing too crazy that's gonna require too much work."

"GW, in and out. 5K for the service."

"Text me the address. And let me change clothes."

"Already did."

"How you knew I was gonna say yes?"

"Cause you have a reputation to uphold. Put your location on."

"Wait, you not coming?" I pulled the phone from my ear to check the time. "Do you see the time? You want me to go by myself?"

"When are you ever alone, Lacey?"

"Umm, Ms. .45 don't count," I said, referring to my gun.

"Lise is having those Braxton Hicks contractions, and I don't wanna leave her side."

Lise was my brother's fiancée, who was carrying their first child. She was well into her third trimester, and after two previous miscarriages, my niece was their miracle baby. My brother was scared to even blink twice when it came to his unborn. I knew they couldn't suffer another loss. Unfortunately, I knew that pain all too well.

"I wouldn't send you nowhere unprotected though. Blind is gonna meet you there and keep watch till you're done."

I sighed. "Alright."

"Sis, you good. And dude is good people."

"Who? The man with the gunshot wound?"

"No. The man who shot him. He's on location too. Hit

me when you leave the house and when you arrive. Love you, sis."

"**Love you too.**" I hung up and stood from the couch. When duty called, I answered.

PULLING UP TO THE 2031 BATHGATE AVENUE address Lance had given me, I spotted my cousin, Blind's Jeep across the street. He flashed his lights twice as a signal that I was good to get out. Checking my medical bag to ensure that I had everything I needed, I proceeded to step out. I'd been a RN for three years and had worked at St. Luke's Hospital in the ER for two of those years. It was a high paced environment, especially overnight, and despite having to deal with an influx of patients every night, I loved my job. While I loved what I did and how I was able to help people from all walks of life, I quickly picked up on how the level of care for my Black and brown people differed from those of palm color.

Always the vocal person, I didn't have a problem voicing my grievances when the time presented itself. Most of the time, what I had to say was met with, "We'll make sure to relay this to upper management," or even just outright taking me off of certain cases. What broke me and made me leave the job I took pride in was when a sixteen-year-old Black kid died due to lack of care.

He'd come in with a gunshot wound to the side with a mob of his friends demanding help for their boy. Their concerns were met with no sense of urgency, and I watched as the young kid was placed on a gurney and pulled into the closest available room.

I'd already made up my mind that I was going to help and took it upon myself to change my assignment so that I was his nurse. I didn't mind dealing with the aftermath later. After taking a quick assessment of his wound, I went to grab everything needed to remove the bullet I felt lodged in his side. I'd just numbed the area to avoid him feeling the pain when the charge nurse snatched the curtain back and demanded that I leave the room.

"Klein, if we don't remove this bullet now in the position it's in, I'm afraid it's going to travel," I spoke through tight lips with one hand on the kid's side and the other holding his shoulder. I could feel him trembling under my touch, but he never said a word.

"I'll take care of it, Alacea. Please go back to your assigned patient. I cannot have you moving in a manner that defies my authority."

I closed my eyes and took a deep breath. Leaning over into the boy's ear, I whispered to him. "I'll be right back in a few minutes. We're gonna get that bullet out and get you fixed up, aight?"

He nodded but still didn't speak. I could see the tears he shed as they hit the pillow, and my heart went out to him.

"Alacea," Nurse Klein spoke again.

Taking a step back, I pulled off my gloves and discarded them before leaving the room to update his crew that had been pushed to the waiting area. When I walked out, they all popped up from their seats.

"Is he good?"

"Can we go back and see him?

"We're having someone take care of him now. Gimme a few for an update, okay?" The look on their faces said they wanted to protest, but they nodded instead.

I went back to my assigned room as instructed, and after assessing the patient's symptoms, I referred him to the on-call doctor who agreed with my diagnosis of the stomach flu. Anxious to get back to the kid, I provided my patient his prescription as well as detailed instructions for aftercare. Finally making my way back to the kid, my heart dropped into the pit of my stomach when I saw him being wheeled out on the hospital bed with the white sheet covering his head. I knew he was gone, and I also knew that had he been given the immediate medical attention I was willing to provide, he would've survived. I coached myself not to cry as I delivered the news to his people. Immediately after, I grabbed my things from the employee locker room and handed my badge to Nurse Klein as I walked out of the emergency room entrance.

I quit that day and told myself that if I was going to aid anyone else in that predicament, it would be the ones who couldn't — or refused to — seek medical attention due to the lives they led. I still had to live, so for the right price, those who played in the streets could get their emergency services through me. I went to my brother, Lance, about my idea, and after a detailed sales pitch, he was on board. His only contingency was that he brought the jobs to me. I was fine with that because the streets were his thing. It had been a year now, and I'd been doing pretty well for myself.

Walking over to Blind's truck, I made sure to be alert in the darkness. He let down the window as I got close, and a cloud of thick smoke engulfed the air, hitting me in the face, sending me into a coughing fit.

"What the fuck, William?! Why would you do that?" I called him by his first name, knowing it would irritate him.

"Aight now. I'm high, and you know how I get when I smoke. Go head with that government name bullshit."

"Whatever. You out here hotboxing like you in *How High* or some shit. Come on. I'm tired, and I wanna be in and out."

"Aight." He took another pull of whatever exotic weed he was smoking and ashed the blunt before getting out of the truck.

"So, do you know this guy?" I questioned as we walked up to the building.

"Yeah. How a nigga supposed to take you serious in a pair of Tweety Bird scrubs, Lacey?"

I shrugged. "So long as the job gets done, it shouldn't matter what I have on. Last I checked, this was Emergency Services, not Fashion 101."

"You got ya shit on you?" he questioned, ignoring my snappy response as always.

I tapped my medical bag. "Ms. .45 at the bottom. .38 on my waist."

Nodding, he pushed the door to the building open, and I followed him to a first floor apartment that had Super written on the door. Blind knocked in code, and I stood at the side of him.

"Who?" The voice on the other end called out.

"Emergency Services," Blind replied.

I only spoke when necessary. For the most part, Lance did all the talking or Blind if he was present. I had a one-track mind when I worked. The door slowly opened, and a Young M.A lookalike stood on the other side of it. I wasn't into women at all, but she was fine.

"Living room. Walk past the first door and make a right," she instructed.

I gave her another once over as I walked past and caught her smirk. She knew she was fine. Following behind Blind, we made it to the living room, and there was a man seated on a couch, rocking back-and-forth, gritting his teeth, clearly holding back tears. My eyes shifted to his hand that was covered with some kind of white cloth with blood seeping out of it.

"Yo, Wiz," the Young M.A lookalike called out to someone.

I heard a toilet flush, followed by running water, before a man emerged from the back of the apartment. When he came into view, my eyes locked in on his, and I felt an aching in between my legs. The fine specimen of a man, who stood over six feet with toffee colored skin and a pleasingly asymmetrical structured face, commanded the room's attention by just his presence alone. The beard with neck tat combo was doing it for me. With alluring eyes that lingered on my face for a few seconds, he then scanned my body before stopping at my medical bag.

"What's good, Blind?"

"Shit. This is Lacey. Lacey, this is Wiz."

"Hey," I spoke.

"Wassup, Beautiful? You need anything?" His voice had a distinct growl to it that was pleasing to my ears.

"Just for y'all to clear the area so I can work. And just to confirm, the bullet went in and out, right?"

"That's correct. And I ain't tryna rush you, Beautiful, but I need him patched up quick, so he can get back to work, and we all can be on our way. Blind and Suge will go. I'll be staying." He casually walked over to the couch, sat next to the guy without acknowledging him, and turned on the TV.

I gave Blind an incredulous look, not believing that this man had just tuned into the stock market while the guy next to him sat bleeding out. The person he called Suge snickered and tapped Blind's shoulder. Blind looked for my signal that I was good, and I nodded the okay for him to leave. I usually didn't like people around me while I worked, but it was clear that he was going to be the exception tonight. Taking out what I needed, I caught Wiz's eye again. I could tell he liked what he saw, and even though I was mad with my man at the moment, I was still off the market. Ending the stare off, I got down to business with every intention of patching this guy up to perfection and adding another 5K to my bank account.

2
WIZ

My plan was to leave the spot after dealing with Slim's stupid ass to avoid shooting him again. I couldn't deal with ignorance, and he knew that, so why he chose to fuck around on the job behooved me. At the last minute, I changed my mind, wanting to meet this nurse face to face. I'd heard nothing but good things about her service, not only in the hood but with those that were in the streets but didn't deal in the day-to-day operations. I happened to tap into the block here and there, so I guess you could say I was a mixture of both. There was no doubt who ran shit though.

I had been referred by one of my homies to Lance and the Emergency Services. He was one of the older street dudes who handled his shit from afar. When my boy, Gritty, mentioned that the on-the-go ER was his thing, I hit him immediately. People had spoken highly of the nurse's professionalism, her punctuality, and most importantly, her ability to keep her mouth closed regarding the dealings of her clientele. No one had ever mentioned her looks though. She was bad.

Her golden skin was clear of any acne, and I didn't see a trace of makeup. I'd had a rotation of women and knew a made-up face when I saw one. Her hair was pulled tightly into a bun that sat on the back of her head, not a single unruly piece escaping the sleek style. I scanned her round eyes and slender nose adorned with a small nose ring that sparkled under the light. It wasn't a hair store nose ring either. I was willing to bet that shorty was rocking a diamond in her shit, and I fucked with that.

I quietly admired her shape and how well she filled out her scrubs. She was thick, the way I liked my women. More than what I could see with my eyes, I enjoyed her silence. She worked quietly for the most part, barely uttering more than a few words to Slim.

"Sssss," Slim hissed audibly. It had been the first time I'd heard his voice since he'd hollered out when I shot him earlier.

"Oh, I'm sorry," Lacey spoke politely. "Let me numb the area a little more."

"Nah," I objected. "He straight. He need to feel every bit of this, so he know not to fucking play on company time again. You straight, right, Slim?" I looked over at him, and he nodded.

"Yeah… Yeah, I'm straight. Just a little stinging, that's all."

I went to turn my attention back to the TV and caught her disapproving look as she shook her head. By the look, I half expected her to say something, but she just went back to what she was doing. Twenty minutes later, she was done and handing Slim two pills.

"Can you get him a glass of water, so he can take these pain pills?"

"What kinda pain pills are those? As I mentioned, he gotta get back to work."

"Just some Ibuprofen. This is 600mg." She focused back on Slim. "You can get some over the counter as well."

"Aight. There's waters in the fridge. You can grab him one."

I watched as her face screwed up, and her forehead creased. "Wiz, right?" I nodded, and she continued. "Yeah, ummm, I don't know what they told you, but I'm not the help. As far as I'm concerned, my job here is done. I was trying to be nice but here you go." She dropped the pills into Slim's now bandaged hand and stood to her feet. "Blind," she called out, and he appeared a few seconds later. "I'm ready." Turning back to me, she held her hand out. "Compensation?"

A smirk rested on my face as I stood to retrieve her money. "Give me a second."

"I'll do you one better and give you sixty."

I chuckled at her slick response as I headed to the kitchen. The money counter had been cleaned of Slim's blood, as it was where he'd sat chilling and smoking as he counted. He was so zoned out and high that he didn't even hear me and Suge come in the apartment. There were rules when money was involved — my money that is. I wanted niggas sober and alert. He wasn't either, and I didn't give him a chance to come up with an excuse before I shot him.

"You're twelve seconds shy of your sixty, sir," Lacey kindly let me know as I picked up the stack I had set aside for her.

Returning to the living room, I placed the money in her open hand. "For your discretion."

She eyed the bills and thumbed through them before placing the stack in her bag. "That's always guaranteed. Thank you."

She turned to Blind, who threw me a head nod, before they made their way to the front door with Suge leading the two. I heard Suge's flirty, "Good night, nurse," and the door closed soon after. She reappeared back in the living room with a slick grin.

"What?" Suge questioned my look.

"Not that one, sis."

"Shit, most definitely. I seen the way shorty was eyeing me at the door and when she left."

"Not that one, sis," I repeated. Suge was known to turn the straightest of women out. I'd seen that shit with my own two eyes. Lacey wasn't gonna be one of them.

"Ahhh, shit. Nigga, you were only around her for forty-five minutes tops."

"It only took me ten to know that I wanna see what she bout."

Suge nodded and conceded with her hands in the air. "All you."

"I'm gone for the night. Stay here till this fuck up finish counting the money and make sure he don't nod off after he take them pills. I'll talk to you in the morning." Dapping her up, I didn't bother addressing Slim.

Leaving the apartment, I hopped in my car and headed straight home with thoughts of who else I could shoot to get a visit from Emergency Services.

THE SOUND OF MY ALARM GOING OFF PULLED ME FROM A restless sleep, alerting me to a presence in my home. Grabbing my gun from the nightstand, I got up just as the person who'd entered deactivated the alarm. The only people who had that code was my mother and my two siblings. Still, you could never be too careful, so I pushed forward with my gun in hand. Turning the corner, I found my sister trying to balance a gallon of water and a paper bag that sat on top of it while managing a conversation with the help of her shoulder to keep her phone from falling.

"How bout you hang up the damn phone, then you can maneuver better?"

"Hold on, bae," she spoke into the phone. "Shut up and come help me, ugly."

Sitting my gun down on the kitchen island, I walked over and grabbed everything from her hand.

"What you used, your nose to put the code in? The phone practically glued to your damn ear."

She waved me off with her hand and focused on her conversation. **"Alright, bae, I'm here. I'll call you later when I'm headed back home. I'll be ready by one. Okay, I will. I love you too."** Ending the call, she grabbed the paper bag and began pulling out its contents. "Keyon said wassup."

"Why you ain't tell me that when he was on the phone?"

She paused and rolled her eyes. "Cause you know how you do witcho rude ass."

"Aight then. Same shit applies whether the nigga on the phone or in my presence. I don't fuck witcho bum."

She slammed a box of Fruity Pebbles down on the island, and her nose flared. "Stop calling him that, Wizdom! I don't say nothing about that skeezer, Fallon, so stop talkin' down on my man."

I wanted to take her seriously but burst out laughing at the skeezer comment. "Nah, skeezer is crazy, Bam."

She couldn't even hold her straight face as she giggled and gave me the finger. "Shut up. You get on my damn nerves. I'm dead not even laughing," she claimed, still giggling. "Put your own shit away."

"Awww, Bam Bam, don't act like that to you brudda." Walking around to where she stood, I bear hugged her and kissed her cheek.

"Ewww, get off me, dirty." Wiggling out of my embrace, she pushed me back.

Two years my junior, Cherish, aka Bam Bam, was the baby of the siblings. While my mother often smothered her growing up, it was my brother, Hakeem, and I whose grasp she couldn't wait to get out of once she was older. Even at this big age of twenty-six, we still made her business our business. And she hated that shit, especially when we expressed our disdain for the type of niggas she claimed.

I'd put the bum title on Keyon after his car broke down in the middle of the night, and she went to rescue him. She claimed that he'd used the last five percent of his battery to call her as opposed to calling AAA. Now, what kind of sense that shit made to her was still confusing till this day, but a bum was what I would continue to refer to him as until I felt different.

"What you doing here?" I questioned, opening the fridge. "Wait, lemme go throw some shorts on."

"Yeah, do that."

Jogging back to my room, I picked up my basketball shorts from the edge of my bed and put them on. As I went to head back to the kitchen, my phone rang. Of the three iPhones that sat on my nightstand, the incoming call came in from my personal phone. Fallon's name dancing across the screen made me smirk, thinking about Cherish calling her a skeezer.

"**Good morning,**" I answered the call on speaker.

"**Hey, baby,**" she sang into the phone. "**How'd you sleep?**"

"**Shit, I can't say. I'm still tired. Why you calling so early?**" Walking back into the kitchen, Cherish had put away whatever groceries she had and was now seated, eating a bowl of cereal.

"**You never called me back yesterday after we hung up.**"

"**My bad. I got caught up in some shit. What you got going on today?**"

"**Ummm, I thought I was chillin' witchu. I bought your nephew a gift for his party today.**"

Cherish's face turned up, and she shook her head no. I didn't recall inviting Fallon to my nephew's party, but I knew she wasn't above ear hustling, so she could've overheard me talking about it on the phone at some point.

"**I appreciate that. And you can slide through. I'll hit you back with a time in a couple hours, cool?**"

"**Yep.**" I could hear the excitement in her voice.

Fallon didn't care where we went or what we did so long as she was able to be seen with me. She was a good fuck, and she wasn't an ugly girl, so I wasn't trippin' about her wanting to be connected to me to portray some kind of status. I'd made it clear that we weren't in a relationship, and she seemed cool with that.

"**Aight. Later, Ma.**"

"**Alright, baby, talk soon.**" She ended the call, and I sat my phone down.

Cherish rolled her eyes and shook her head.

"What, crazy?"

"I know my nephew is on his way to being famous with

this modeling that he has going on, but there are no groupies allowed at this party."

"Girl, shut up."

"No. You have a problem with Keyon being around, and I have a problem with Fallon tryna use my nephew's party as a photo op."

"Well, the difference between me and you is you know I ain't going for that."

"Whatever." She rolled her eyes again and continued eating.

"You so childish." I chuckled. "Mama told you to come over here?"

"No. I was in Trader Joe's and decided to bring you some stuff. You know if it wasn't for me and Mommy, you'd probably starve."

Opening the fridge, I grabbed a bottle of water. "Nah, if it wasn't for you, Mommy, and Uber Eats, I'd starve. Preciate you thinkin' of me though, sis."

"Yeah, yeah, whatever. Ahhh, man." She picked up her phone with a disappointed look.

"What?"

"Nothing. I invited my friend to the party, and now, she's claiming to be under the weather. Let me call this girl."

Shrugging my shoulders, I sat up on the counter and went through the unanswered messages on my phone.

"Ughh, do you mind?" She cocked her head to the side and pointed to her phone that was now ringing on speakerphone.

"Bam, this my shit. Ain't nobody worried about your little conversation. Take the call off speaker."

Giving me the finger for the second time since she'd arrived, she spoke into the phone as it connected.

"How you under the weather when you were just fine last night, girl?"

"I'm just tired, Cherish." I heard a familiar voice say, followed by a yawn. **"I wanna chill today."**

"Nah, that nigga done did something and blew your mood. Come out today please. You know you wanna see your lil' man. He asked if you were coming to his party. Don't do my nephew like that, Lacey."

"Ahh, how you gon' pull that card knowing how I feel about my lil' boo?" I could hear her suck her teeth and sigh. **"Alrighttt. The only reason I'm coming is for Dooty. I got his gift, and I don't want him to have to wait for it. I'm not staying long though."**

Cherish clapped with a satisfied grin on her face. **"Yayyy. Love you. See you at two."**

"Yeah, yeah, love you too, chick. Bye." The call ended, and I hopped down off the counter.

"Who dat?"

"My friend, Alacea. Why, nosey?"

"Oh, aight, just askin'. I'm bout to head back to sleep for a few hours. Wash that dish before you leave."

"I can't wait not to do it!" she yelled out as I walked back to my bedroom.

Closing my door behind me, I laid back down with my

hands behind my head, looking up at the ceiling. It was no coincidence that Bam knew a Lacey, and I was just introduced to one this morning. It wasn't a common name. I could've pressed for more info, but if she planned to be at the party, a formal introduction was bound to happen. She'd met Wiz, the bully; now, she'd have the pleasure of meeting Wizdom, the family man.

3
ALACEA

I'd gone back to sleep after Cherish called and woke up a little after twelve in the afternoon to no missed calls or texts from Quan. I was so frustrated that I wanted to cry. The least he could've done after flaking on me last night was keep his word today. It was shit like this that made me wonder why I even bothered. Sitting up on the couch where I'd replanted myself after coming back home this morning, I grabbed my phone to text Ashlynn.

Me: Hey, I know you probably still annoyed with me but just reaching out to see if you were going to Dooty's party today.

Ash: ...Yeah. I just got off the phone with Cherish. You goin?

Me: Yeah. You wanna ride together?

I was hoping she said yes. In order to not have Quan and

his bullshit on my brain, I needed to be engaged with other people.

Ash: We can do that. You coming to me, or you want me to come to you?

Me: 😊. I can come to you. Give me an hour to get myself together.

Ash: Cool. Just text when you get here, and I'll come down so that we're not super late.

Me: Got it.

I went to lock my phone when it rang in my hand. I rolled my eyes in disgust seeing Quan's name pop up on the screen. Hitting the decline button, I kept moving toward my bedroom. The phone rang again, and this time, I answered.

"Hey," I spoke dryly.

"Hey, baby."

"Wassup?"

"I just wanted to call and tell you I love you. I'm sorry about last night."

"This morning too?"

"Yeah, I overslept. I didn't get in till late. I actually just woke up a few minutes ago. How'd you sleep?"

I sensed that some fuck shit was amiss and couldn't shake it. Going with that feeling, I responded. "I didn't get much sleep. Where'd you rest your head last night because I'm outside of your building, and I don't see your car."

"Huh? Outside where?"

"In front of your building. I was about to come up when you called, but like I said, I don't see your car."

"Oh, I let..." The sounds of a baby crying cut him off, making my brow shoot up. It was the second time I'd heard a baby in his background, this time clearer than the last.

"Whose baby is that?" I questioned, only to be met with dead air. Pulling the phone from my ear, I checked the screen that now displayed my wallpaper. "I know damn well this nigga didn't just hang up on me." I went to dial his number back when a voice in my head commanded me to stop. What was done in the dark would always come to the light. Another voice said, *Bitch, you are the light. Find out what that nigga up to.*

I always made sure to share my location when I was out, and Quan would do the same, even if it was only for an hour max. While I was open to doing so in the event of an emergency, I knew he only went along with it to appease me temporarily. As I navigated the settings in our texts, I only hoped that he was so preoccupied with his "business" last night that he'd clicked the always share button on accident. And as luck would have it, he had, and the location of his phone damn sure wasn't his apartment. It was his mother's house.

It did nothing to alter my suspicion though. Why would anyone go out of their way to lie about being at their mother's house? The shit just didn't make any sense. Instead of starring in a real live version of *Clue*, I called him back. Surprisingly, he answered on the first ring.

"My bad, bae. My phone died. I had to plug it up to a charger."

"Are you home?"

"Nah. I crashed at my mom's. Her house is closer to where I was, and I was dead tired, so I knew I wouldn't have made it home without falling asleep at the wheel."

I wanted to believe him, but the nagging feeling in my gut wouldn't let me, so I gave a simple response. "Oh, okay. I heard a baby in the background this morning and just before the phone disconnected."

"Yeah, my mother is babysitting for my cousin, and you know Quaid got a son. When I went to scoop him last night, lil' man was up and shit. Lil' one got some pipes on 'em, don't he? I can't wait for you to pop out a mini me."

What were the odds that I'd heard the same baby cries at two different times? Something wasn't adding up, and something in me knew that if I kept pressing the issue, Quan would just get more creative with his responses, so I accepted what he said.

"Okay."

"Bae, don't be like that. I'ma make up for last night. I promise. Matter fact, let's do something today. I'll push business back, and it'll just be me and you."

Any other time, that would've sounded like music to my ears, but this wasn't one of those times. Quan needed to understand that my time was just as valuable as his and needed to be respected just as much.

"Today won't be good. I have plans."

"What plans? And why am I just now finding out?"

"Well, I figured since last minute is your thing, me telling you now shouldn't be an issue."

Entering my bedroom, I went straight for my closet to find something to wear.

"Aight, man. You wanna be on that petty shit. I'm just tryna make shit right."

"Stop being wrong then you don't have to try and make shit right all the time. You ever thought about that?"

"Yeah, I'ma go. Hope you have a good day. I love you."

"Uh huh. Love you too." I ended the call and tossed my phone on the bed.

I quickly picked out an outfit suitable for a child's birthday party and went to the shower. I wanted nothing more than to lay back down, but I'd given my word and didn't want to give the girls any more reason to throw salt on my relationship. Quan was doing an A1 job at proving them right as it was.

To put me in a better mood, I turned on YouTube and selected my Glorilla Summer '24 playlist. One thing I could count on was my girl to put me in a fuck that nigga mood, even if I knew it was temporary.

It's 7 p.m. Friday. It's 95 degrees. I AIN'T GOT NO NIGGA AND NO NIGGA AIN'T GOT ME!

PULLING UP TO THE PARK WHERE CHERISH'S NEPHEW'S PARTY was going on, my jaw almost hit the steering wheel. The park was sprawling with kids, and by the setup, I could see why. From the street, I could see three bouncy houses set up, one equipped with a water slide. The kids were having a grand ol' time.

"Oh, they not fuckin' around," Ashlynn commented. "I wish I had AJ with me this weekend." AJ was her three-year-old son who she shared custody of with her ex-husband.

"I know, right? Did you ask to alternate with Tim?"

"Yep, and soon as he started to make the conversation about us, I ended the call. You know I'm not beat for the bullshit. I be quick to hang up on a nigga."

I snickered, knowing she told no lies. "This I know. Come on. Let's get out. The icee man just pulled up, and I want me a little coco, cherry, mango." I mimicked the Spanish guys that pushed the icee carts around in the summer, making Ashlynn laugh.

We both stepped out of the car and grabbed our gifts from my trunk. Entering the park, I quickly took notice that what we saw from the street was only a snippet of what they really had going on. There was a candy station, a nerf gun wall, face painting, and all kinds of shit. Everything went right in with the theme of Dayton's Playhouse.

"Oh, my God, I'm so glad y'all made it," Cherish said, making a quick jog over to us. "Save me please! If my mama asks me to do one more thing, I'ma lose my shit."

"Hey, girl." I giggled. "You look cute." She had on a pair of jean shorts and a cut up t-shirt that had "Dooty's Fav Aunt" spray painted on it

"You are a fuckin' mess. How you his favorite aunt, and you his only aunt, Cherish?" Ashlynn commented with a laugh and gave her a hug.

"I'm his only aunt on his daddy side. He got two on his mama side. I wanted to let them hoes know what's really going on, especially the one who ain't get here yet that's always poppin' that shit bout my brother. And how bout the man who did the shirt messed up? It was actually supposed to say his favorite person."

"And survey says, that's a lie," I chimed in. "Cause we know that's me. Where's lil' handsome anyway? I wanna give him his gift."

"My brother just took him to the bathroom to change out of his swimsuit. Come on. You can put your gifts on the gift table, then we gon' grab us a drink from the adult cooler." She grinned and linked her arm with Ashlynn's.

"Here, take mine." I handed her the two gift bags I held. "I wanna go get me an icee real quick."

"Girl, we got a whole snack bar." She pointed over to the snack area set up under a tent with all kinds of candy, cakes, and pastries.

"I intend to make a pit stop there after I eat. Right now, this icee is calling my name. I'll find y'all."

Turning away from them to head back to the park's entrance, I hoped that the guy hadn't waddled off. As I walked out of the gate, I heard my name called by a small voice.

"Laceyyyy!" Spinning around, I saw Dooty bolting

toward me at high speed. I laughed, bending down with my arms open for him to run into my embrace.

"Birthday mannn!!!" I greeted, matching his excitement and giving him a tight hug. "Why you ain't tell me you were having a water slide? I would've brought my bathing suit."

He took a step back and shrugged his shoulders. "Ion know. It was here when I got here. Uncle Wiz don't have one either."

I looked up just in time to see the guy from this morning approaching us with a friendly smile.

"Oh, hey. I didn't think I'd see you again, and not at a kid's party."

"Same," he replied. "You look good, Beautiful."

I gave my jean romper a quick scan and agreed. "Thank you."

"Can you get me an icee, Uncle Wiz?" Dooty asked.

"I was just going to get one myself," I said. "If you don't mind, I can get his."

"How about I buy both of y'alls?" he offered.

"Okay." Thinking nothing of it, we walked over with Dooty in the middle of us, ordered our icees, and went back to the party. Dooty took off once Wiz gave him the go ahead.

"That boy gon' fuck that Off White fit up."

"Bad," I concurred, giggling. "Thanks for the icee. I knew Cherish had two brothers; I wouldn't have guessed you were one of them."

"Yeah, her and Keem have the same pops, so they look

most alike, while I share my mama's good genes. I'm like David Ruffin, and they The Temptations type shit."

We both laughed at him lowkey calling his siblings ugly. "You wrong." I took two licks of the top layer of the icee and savored the coconut flavor. "This is so good. How's that guy's hand?"

"Couldn't tell you. I haven't spoken to him."

"Oh, okay. He's gotta be careful about his movement. So, light duty only if he can manage it. If you need me to, I can check on the stitches in about a week to make sure it's healing properly. There's no charge."

"Why?"

"Why what?"

"Why wouldn't you charge? If he had to be seen at the hospital for a follow-up after a procedure, they'd charge his insurance. You do the same."

"And you being his employer, I'll be charging you."

"That's correct. And that medical insurance will come out of his pay. We all win round here."

I laughed at his logic. "I guess you're right."

"Even when I'm wrong."

"Oh, hey, I see you've met my brother. Was he nice?" Cherish approached us and stood next to me.

"Yes, he was nice. He bought me this icee. This is actually our second time meeting. He wasn't so nice at the first intro-duction."

"Man, that's cap," Wiz let out.

"You told me to go fetch some water."

He chuckled, and I smiled. "Why you lyin'?"

"Alright, I'm stretching the truth a bit."

"Exactly."

"Well, cool, glad y'all met but I'ma take my friend now. Yours is walking in." Cherish pointed to the entrance where there was a tall, yellow woman walking in the park with balloons and a gift bag. "Bringing a bunch of balloons to a birthday party like there isn't balloons here already is so goofy by the way."

I snickered as she grabbed my hand, and he waved at me as we walked off. It was cute, and I found myself waving back.

"My brother like you. And if you still have hope for your relationship with ol' boy, you better make him unlike you and quick." I laughed at the expression on Cherish's face as we trekked up the small hill to get to the main festivities.

"Girl, what? I've only known of your brother's existence for a few hours."

"And I've known him for twenty-six years, boo. Trust me when I say that Wizdom is coming for you, and he don't give no fucks bout no nigga in his way."

"Okay. I'll keep that in mind."

Cherish was tripping, and what she was saying really went in one ear and out the other. Yeah, her brother was fine as hell and seemed cool, but that was about it. I had a man, and despite my doubts, part of me still felt like I could maintain the relationship so long as we were on the same page and Quan could stop the fuck shit.

"Ooouu, I can't wait to see how this plays out." She rubbed her hands together, and I waved her off, finding my eyes shifting back in the direction of Wiz.

While the woman stood in front of him, talking, he stared directly at me. I watched as he discreetly nodded before focusing back on her. I didn't know what that was about but didn't let it rent space in my head.

"Once I finish this icee, we going in the bouncy house," I let Cherish know.

"Well, hurry up cause Ash is already in there." We both laughed, knowing our big asses were about to take over the five-year-old birthday party with no shame.

4

WIZ

"This is a nice setup. Where should I put his gift and the balloons?"

I heard Fallon talking, but I was too busy watching my sister and Lacey climb into the ball pit with the kids. Smirking, I shook my head. I could hear the kids yelling at them to get out before they started tossing the balls back-and-forth.

"Wiz."

"Yeah."

"I asked where I should put the balloons and your nephew's gift?"

"Oh, here, lemme get the bag. I'll put it on the gift table. You can put the balloons in the air. I'll reimburse you." I didn't know what she was thinking bringing them, but it didn't make sense at all.

"In the air?"

"Yeah. It's kinda wild to bring balloons to a birthday party, don't you think? Especially when that wasn't requested of you. Unless your intention was to gain some kinda points."

"I didn't think of it that way. And it would look crazy for me to let the balloons go in the middle of the party, Wiz."

I shrugged. "Suit yourself." If she wanted to be the topic of conversation, and not for good reason, then so be it.

"Ooouu, let's take a picture real quick, bae." Fallon stood in front of me and pulled out her phone. Before she could get to the camera, I stopped her.

"Ay, we not doing that. This day is about my nephew. You're either here to be present or we can link another day."

"You're right." Sliding her phone back into her purse, she went to grab my hand.

I wasn't the holding hands type, so I ain't know what she was on. I wrapped my arm around her neck and kissed her forehead. "Stop actin' weird, man. Be present. It's a party for a five-year-old. We bout to play a few games, run after these kids, and eat."

"I don't know how much running I'm gonna be doing in this dress, but I'm here for the fun."

I snickered. "Aight."

Walking over to one of the tents my mother had set up for the adults, I placed the gift on the table amongst the others. Though I had no plans to sit up under Fallon for the duration of the party, I wanted my people to know that she was with me and she was straight.

"Wizdom, why you bought Dooty an icee when we done spent all this money on that snack table?" my mother fussed from where she sat with my aunts.

"That two dollars I spent ain't gon' break the bank, and it ain't gon' stop him from running over to that snack table, Ma. Let him enjoy his day."

"Let him enjoy his day my ass. You ain't the one Hakeem gon' drop him off to later. He get to running up and down my marble wood floors like he Sonic The Hedgehog and we gon' be at yo' door tonight."

I laughed because knowing my mother, she would literally pull up to my crib at two in the morning with no problem.

"Aight, my bad. This is Fallon, y'all. Fallon, this my mother, Queen, and my aunts, Dotty and Maxine."

"Nice to meet you all." Fallon waved, and they did the same.

"Hey, love," my mother spoke. "Wizdom, take those balloons and tie them to one of the chairs, so she don't have to hold them." I did as she instructed and tied them to one of the chairs under the tent. "Look at these big ass kids. Your sister and them know they better not come over here spraying that damn water."

I turned just in time to see Cherish and Lacey creeping up with wide grins and two Super Soaker water guns in their hands.

"Cherish, I promise you if you spray me with that water..."

"Boy, shut up. I'm not even gon' spray you," she interrupted.

"I am," Lacey confessed before wetting me up with the gun.

Cherish burst out laughing. "Run, Lacey!" she shouted, and they took off, but I was right on her heels.

Her ass must've run track in school because she was booking it, but I was gon' get my lick back, so I kept up speed with us eventually passing Cherish and ending up by the swings.

"I'm sorry. I'm sorry," she said between giggles. "It was a dare. I'm sorry."

"Nah, you done fucked up."

She went to fake a right, but I was onto her, swooping her up in my arms as she tried to run past me. She was laughing so hard that she snorted, which made me laugh.

"You wetting up my outfit, Wizdom! Put me down!"

"Nope! You shouldn't have let her talk you into this. Y'all wanna play, let's play." Running back down the hill with her yelling the whole way, I couldn't stop laughing.

"Alrighttt, you got it. You got it. I'll give you whatever you want if you put me down. I'ma bout to pee on myself."

"Well, the water from the sprinklers gon' get you right." I wasn't gonna put her in the water, but she didn't know that.

"Noooo!" By now, we were back at the party area and nearing the sprinklers. She buried her face in my shirt and kicked her legs. "Wizdom!! Don't!"

"Aight, say you sorry again and that you'll let me take you out to breakfast tomorrow."

Her head popped up. "What? No."

"Cool, this water bout to cool you off from this heat."

"Waitt!!! Okay, deal. Just put me down."

"That's your word?"

She looked up at me and smiled. "Yes. I'm sorry, and that's my word."

Nodding, I let her down on her feet, and she straightened her shorts that had risen up a little. "Sike!" she yelled out before bolting across the park.

I chuckled, shaking my head. "Oh, you going," I said out loud to myself before jogging back over to the tent where I'd left Fallon. By the look on her face, I could tell she was in her feelings.

"Wiz!" I heard my brother call out to me. I held my finger up, signaling for him to give me a minute.

"You good?" I asked Fallon, whose lip was curled up in a scowl.

"Shit, I know I wouldn't be. And if she say she is, she silly as hell," my Aunt Dotty commented.

"Mind yo' business, Dotty. Them is two grown people. And he wasn't talkin' to you." My mother cut her eye at her sister, who shook her head. My mama was gon' step behind me right, wrong, or indifferent.

"Can I talk to you over here please?" Fallon requested, gesturing with her head for us to walk out of the tent. I followed behind her, a few feet away, until we were out of earshot of my people.

"Wassup?"

"Did you invite me here to embarrass me, Wiz? Cause that shit you just pulled is really crazy to me. How you just leave me standing there with your family looking all lost?"

"Technically, I didn't invite you. You invited yourself. But I ain't trippin'. We here to have a good time. Anything else, I ain't beat for. So, what you doin'?"

"I'm just saying… I'm here with you. I don't expect to be left alone."

"Well, move when I move then, Fallon. If you ain't tryna do that, cool. We can chill another time."

"That's not what I said."

"Wiz!" I heard my name again. Looking up, I saw Cherish waving me over. "Come on. We taking pictures with the birthday boy."

"Aight, here I come!" Turning back to Fallon, I waited for her to make a decision on what she wanted to do. "You staying or you leaving?"

Sucking her teeth, she rolled her eyes. "I'ma just head out. I hope your nephew likes his gift."

I nodded. "Cool. Preciate you pullin' up. Enjoy the rest of your day."

Kissing her cheek, I wished her safe travels and jogged over to the photo booth we had set up. I wasn't into ass kissing, and I damn sure wasn't gonna beg Fallon to stay if she didn't wanna be here. She'd made the best decision for herself in the end because if I was being real, I was on Lacey's head, and I wasn't hiding it.

5

ALACEA

If my air-dried romper and frizzy curls were any indication of how much fun I was having at this kid party, then my permanent smile said it all. Me and Cherish had completely taken over while Ash seemed to find herself everywhere Cherish's brother, Hakeem, seemed to be. I picked up on it immediately, making sure to watch my cousin's back from afar. Dooty's mother and her family were in attendance, and although Cherish confirmed that there was nothing going on between the two besides healthy co-parenting, I wanted to be cautious.

"Girl, I'm going to get a bottle of water. You want one? These kids out here tryna kill me." I laughed at Cherish as she bent over with her hands on her knees, trying to catch her breath after all the running we'd done.

"Yeah. With all that running, I done worked up an appetite." I rubbed my stomach, excited to sit down and eat.

"I know. Me too. My mama made… I know you fuckin' lyin' to me." Her eyes got wide, and she shot up straight.

"What?" She was no longer looking at me but past me.

She didn't respond verbally, but by the way her eyes turned into slits and she shook her head, I knew something was wrong, so I turned around. She couldn't have prepared me for what I saw if she wanted to. I watched as Quan walked up the hill with an infant in his arms, while a woman walked beside him, pushing a stroller. The surge of heat that went through my body scared me. I wanted to move, but I was stuck in place.

"Don't even trip, friend. We bout to jump that nigga and beat that bitch ass. Hol' on." Cherish was hype behind me, but I couldn't even focus on her with my eyes glued to Quan.

The way he held the baby close to his chest, the connection was evident. While I stared at the two who made their way over to the cake table not too far from us, I turned my head quickly so that he wouldn't spot me. I didn't know who the woman was, and though I wanted to waltz over and find out, I didn't want to embarrass myself.

"We gon' put these water guns to the side. Here, wrap your hair up." She held out a black scrunchie for me. "I don't know where Ashlynn is, but she'll hear us and come running."

"I'm not gonna make a scene out here with all these kids,

Cherish. I'm not about to be out here looking crazy, although I do wanna fuck him up."

"A scene? Girl, we bout to make a fuckin' movie out this bitch! His disrespectful ass gon' learn today. Out in public with the next bitch. He got some fuckin' nerve! Oh, here come Ashlynn now."

Ashlynn stormed our way, and my hope that she hadn't seen Quan before I was able to tell her he was present was dead. I went to say something to her and stopped when I heard Cherish's mother call for everyone to come say happy birthday.

"I'm gonna address it, y'all, but not here. Chill." The two of them were more pissed than me, and it was my dude that had me out here looking stupid. I was so shocked, and I was scared of my reaction. Me calming the two of them down was really me coaching myself too.

"Alright, we'll do it your way," Ashlynn stated calmly. "I'm telling you now, if you keep fuckin' with that nigga after today, you can count on me to not be around much. I refuse to sit back and watch you let a nigga fumble your heart."

"DAMN RIGHT, TREY SONGZ!"

"If my head wasn't fucked up right now, that shit would've been funny, but I hear y'all. Let's go sing happy birthday, so I can go."

They both stood at my side, and we walked over to where the crowd had gathered around the cake table. After assuring them I was good with a nod of my head, I did my best to maneuver the people, so I wouldn't be seen, only to end up bumping into Wiz's back.

"Shoot, my bad." I offered my apology while glancing behind me and walking on the other side of him. I figured I could use his six-foot height as a shield.

"You good," he assured me. "Who you hiding from?"

"Huh?"

"Huh," he mimicked. "I said who you hiding from?"

"Nobody. Sing happy birthday," I encouraged with a nudge of my shoulder.

We sang the Black version of the happy birthday song, followed by melodic hand claps that had the crowd going. I found it commendable how Dooty's parents were able to stand side by side in celebration of him. I smiled at the excitement etched on his face, but the smile soon faded when the realization that my "man" was at this same celebration with what could be his secret family. As they started to cut the cake, I figured it would be the best time to make my exit, only I was too slow. I took one step and locked eyes with Quan, who looked like he'd seen a ghost.

I didn't know what my face was doing, but my heartrate had quickened, and I could feel the tears burning my eyes and a scream in my throat. It felt as if everyone in the park had disappeared, and it was just me and him. And for a minute, I forgot that wasn't the case until I felt a presence next to me and remembered that Wiz hadn't moved.

"Whatever it is, you better not let a muhfucka see you cry in this park, Beautiful," he said.

I didn't know why, but his statement made me do the exact opposite. Hot tears trickled down my face, and my chest collapsed when Quan turned his back to me.

"Come on." Without waiting for my permission, Wiz grabbed my hand and gently pulled me toward the park's exit.

With my head down, I kept up with his pace, dazed by the silent interaction between Quan and I. It was one thing to have a feeling that you were being played, but to see it up close and personal was a different kind of hurt. Realizing that we were now out of the park, I stopped midstep.

"Wait. Where are you taking me?"

"To my car so you can get right."

"I'm good." I sniffled.

"Yeah, well, your tears say different. This me, get in." He hit the locks on an all-black Benz.

"I can't."

"I insist. And I ain't gotta get in there witchu. I don't want these people to see you out here crying though. Get in, get your bearings, and I'ma call my sister and let her know you with me. If you want her and your other homegirl to come sit witchu, that's fine, or if you need an ear, I can be that too."

Opening the passenger side door, he gestured for me to get in. Hesitantly, I got inside and slid into the leather seat. As soon as the door closed, the waterworks started, and I couldn't stop them. I felt crazy crying in a stranger's car, but the betrayal and hurt I was feeling could no longer be contained. It was a good thing that I made the last minute decision not to wear makeup today because I was sure I looked too ugly at the moment and would've looked a mess with mascara running down my face. In an attempt to compose myself, I took deep breaths in and slowly let them out. Hearing my phone ring in my purse, I pulled it out, and upon seeing Quan's name, my hands shook. I wanted to hear what his bitch ass had to say, so I answered.

"Hello."

"Where you at? I'm standing at your car. We need to talk." His tone was calm, almost like he was being mindful of what he said.

"Do you have a baby?" I questioned, not bothering to beat around the bush.

"Alacea, bae... I..."

"Do... you... have... a... fuckin'... baby... NayQuan? Yes or no?" My voice was low but menacing as I spoke through gritted teeth.

"Yes, but..."

"How old is the baby?" Balling my hand into a fist, my leg jumped up and down at a rapid pace.

"He's six months."

I scoffed and wiped my remaining tears. I couldn't give his bitch ass the satisfaction of even hearing me whimper. **"Six months,"** I repeated. **"I wanted to give you the benefit of the doubt. I really did because contrary to what you've shown me time and time again, I wanted to believe that there was a cutoff to how far you'd go. You don't love me, Quan. You love what I bring to the table. You love how I'm**

coming about you. It must do something good to yo' ego to know that you have — excuse me, had — that kind of access to my heart."

"Lacey, I..."

"No, let me get this out because it'll be the last time you'll ever hear me so much as breathe again. Understand that you only get one me in a lifetime, and when you fuck up, you gotta live with seeing me move on cause, please believe, that's exactly what I'ma do. I wish you and your new family we... wait, no the fuck I don't. I wish you hell, nigga. I hope that baby keep yo' ass up with all that crying, and it affect yo' sleep so bad ya bitch ass walk around delirious for months from sleep deprivation. Clear my line and get the FUCK from in front of my car!"

Just as I hit the end button on my phone, there were two knocks at the window. I turned to the driver's side where Wiz now stood. He gestured toward the locks, and I nodded, letting him know it was okay for him to enter his own car. Once inside, he started it up and put the air on. Reaching over me, he popped open the glove compartment and handed me a few tissues.

"Thank you."

"No sweat. How long you been crying?"

His question was odd and made me feel crazy that I'd even let him see my tears. "Umm... I don't know how to answer that. I didn't time myself." Using the tissues to wipe the remnants of any tears, I placed them in my bag to discard later. "I don't mean to be rude, but that's kind of a weird question, don't you think?"

He shook his head. "Depending on if you're answering the question on a surface level. I'm not asking how long you've been crying today, Beautiful. I wanna know how long you've been crying in general."

I paused to let his question sink in, wondering why a man whom I'd only known a few hours would ask such a question. The tone and intent behind the question let me know that there was no malice in it, and it wasn't off base. I just wanted to know why he was inclined to know. Even with all that going through my head, I answered honestly.

"Long enough."

He nodded. "I think you should do something about that."

"You're not the only one. Thanks for letting me hide out in your car for a few." Placing my hand on the door handle, I went to step out.

"Ay."

"Yeah?" I turned my head slightly toward him.

"You know the best way to get over an old nigga?"

I smiled a little. "No, how?"

He licked his lips, and my smile grew wider. "Get up under a real one."

Shaking my head, I let out a giggle and exited the car. Wiz was a witty one, but there just might've been some truth in his statement. I wasn't pressed to find out until I fully detoxed myself of Quan though. And I planned to start tonight.

I'M F R E E FUCK NIGGA FREE!

6

WIZ

I tried to skate off once the party was done, but Cherish's big mouth ass called me out, and now I was on clean up and breakdown duty along with my brother and a few of my cousins. It would've been a quick and easy process had we not been under the direction of my Aunt Dotty who'd had one drink too many.

"Nephew, you gotta tilt the table a lil' bit then fold the legs. Here, lemme show you."

My cousin, Teka, let out a frustrated sigh as she walked over to us. "Ma, he got it. Come on. You doing too much. Sit down. I'ma bout to take you home." She knew how her mother could get after one too many red cups, so she made sure to monitor her intake at all family events.

"I'm good, Auntie. Thank you." I mouthed to Teka that she was cool, and she nodded in response.

"Ay, bruh, I ain't seen yo ass all day." My brother made his way over to me, and I took in his appearance. This nigga hadn't broken a sweat, which meant he wasn't working.

"Why is it that I'm out here working like a Hebrew slave, and my son ain't have no party?"

He shrugged and took a sip of his bottled water. "Cause you don't have a son, bruh."

"Mannn, you got me fucked up. You betta get yo ass over here and help." He laughed and picked up the other side of the table that I was folding. "And the reason you ain't seen me all day is cause you was too busy sniffing behind Cherish homegirl. You ain't low."

I'd watched the way Keem and Ashlynn had managed to occupy the same spaces throughout the party. I wasn't mad at him though.

"Don't say that shit too loud. You know how yo' sister get about her friends, man."

"How I get?" Cherish appeared out of nowhere and stood behind Keem with her hand on her hip.

"How she always do that shit, bruh?" he asked me.

"Do what?" Cherish answered.

"Pop up outta no-damn-where when we're talkin' about you. You been doing that shit since we were kids," I responded. "Watch out so we can move this table."

She stepped back and walked alongside us. "It's a gift that Mama passed down. Back to how I get though, Keem."

"Overprotective of yo friends like a nigga gon' do sum'n to em' that they ain't gon' like."

"And more than once," I added, and we laughed. Cherish didn't find that shit funny at all. Her lip curled up in a scowl, making Keem suck his teeth.

"Stop being so sensitive, Bam," he coddled. "You know we just fuckin' witchu."

"And that's the exact reason I don't want my friends entertaining y'all. Y'all just wanna fuck."

"Girl, they grown as fuck. They don't need you to make no decisions for them. And stop actin' like that's all we be on. We were raised in the same household. You know Mama ain't going for us treating women any kind of way." Keem's face now matched hers, showing he was offended by her statement.

"Yeah, we only fuck the skeezers. We court and eventually wife the good women," I added.

"Yo, what the hell is a skeezer, bruh?"

I laughed and looked to Cherish. "Ask Bam. She called Fallon one this morning. That shit had me dying laughing."

She held her hand up to her mouth to hide that she was giggling too. "Shut up, Wizdom. I'm not saying y'all are bad men at all. Y'all are my brothers, so I know y'all were raised right. At the same time, I haven't seen either of you settle down with one woman yet. Wiz, you like Fallon but not on a "lets be together" level. And Keem, you didn't even try to make it work with Kenya after y'all had Dooty. My girls are great women, and I want the best for them just like they want for me."

"The fuck?" Now I was offended.

"Oh, my God, not like that. Let me rephrase."

"Yeah, cause you got me fucked up, Bam."

"Let's just say y'all get together and it don't work out. I don't wanna lose my friends. I really love those girls like sisters, but y'all my brothers, and it's us over everything and everyone. Y'all get what I'm saying?"

Me and Keem looked at each other then back at her. "Nope," we said in unison.

"Ain't nobody tryna fuck on yo homegirls and leave them. Damn, can we get to know them a lil' bit?" Keem spoke.

Cherish sucked her teeth. "Y'all gon' do what y'all wanna do anyway. All I'm saying is y'all better do right, or I'ma tell Mama."

We laughed at the pout on her face.

"Yeah, aight. Slide me Ashlynn's number," Keem requested. "I forgot to ask her when she left. I was so busy running behind son son."

"And gimmie Lacey's address and her phone number."

"Her address?" Cherish repeated.

"Yeah. Don't trip. I'ma text her before I pull up. I'm definitely pulling up though."

"Oh, Lord. Don't make me regret putting y'all on please."

"I got you, Bam Bam. I ain't gon' make you look bad. Now, come on. Let's hurry up with this so a nigga can head home. Text me the info."

I could see the hesitation in Cherish's face, but she did as we requested before walking off. I meant what I said about not making her look bad. After seeing Lacey cry today, I was gon' be the nigga to put a smile on her face going forward.

It was a little after 9 p.m. when I left the park and headed home. I didn't think a kid party would have me worn out, but all that running around had a nigga beat. I was ready to shower and chill for the night. As I got closer to home, Lacey crossed my mind. I didn't know where her head was after she had her moment earlier, and now that I had her number, I felt compelled to hit her up. Pulling out my phone, I went to the text thread with Cherish where she'd sent the number and proceeded to text Lacey.

Me: Beautiful, I hope you're feeling better than you were earlier. Don't be mad at Bam for giving me your number. I kinda talked her out of it. 😏

Not knowing if she'd answer or not, I went to set my phone down in the cupholder when a message from Fallon came through.

Fallon: Hey, you up for some company?

I thought about her question before typing my response. I was up for some company but not Fallon's. At the same time, I knew her encrypted text didn't reference actual chilling. Asking if I was up for some company was Fallon's way of telling me she wanted some dick. I wasn't the type of person you could just pop up on, and she knew that early on. I had to be in the mood to deal with your presence, hence the reason for her text. I guess I was taking too long to respond because she followed up with the tongue and eggplant emoji. Nasty shit like that made my dick hard.

Me: You sure know how to get a nigga in yo bed. I'm on my way. Keep it drippin' fa me.

Fallon: Yes, Daddy.

I smirked at her response because she was laying it on thick. Turning my car in the opposite direction of my house, I headed to hers. Checking my message to Lacey, I saw that she'd read the message but still hadn't responded. I wasn't trippin'. She'd be seeing me in the morning for the breakfast date she thought she was getting out of. When I wanted something, it was mine, and there wasn't a discussion to be had about it. And while I didn't know much of anything about her yet, she had an aura about her that made me want to explore more.

I was so caught up in my thoughts that I didn't hear my burner phone going off. I knew it was Suge, and I had a feeling that whatever she was calling about was sure to blow me. I could sense these things.

"What's the word, Suge?"

"Ay, man, this nigga, Slim, done hit his hand and bust the stitches shorty put in."

I sighed and pinched the bridge of my nose. **"How you know that, Suge?"**

"Cause I'm standing here in front of his goofy ass rocking back-and-forth, and that bandage she put on got blood all in it. You gotta hit ol' girl."

Though I wanted to punch Slim in his shit for whatever careless shit he did to bust the stitches, being able to link

71

with Lacey again was the only consolation for the bill he would incur.

"**Aight, man. I'll call her and get her over there.**"

I could hear Suge snicker. "**Oh, you gon' call her directly? What happened to reaching out to Lance?**"

"**Stop clocking my moves, Miss.**"

"**Ay, chill with that 'miss' shit. And ain't nobody clockin' you, Speedy. Go for what you know, my boy.**"

"**I plan to. Gimmie a minute and I'll be there. Make sure that nigga don't get to bleeding all over the place.**"

"**Got you.**"

The line disconnected, and I called Lacey. The phone rang a couple times on my end before it went to voicemail. Persistent, I didn't let the unanswered call deter me and called again. This time, she answered on the first ring.

"**Hello,**" she answered with a sniffle.

"**You crying again?**"

"**No,**" she lied.

"**Ay, don't do that shit, Beautiful.**" My tone was stern.

"**Do what?**"

"**Lie.**"

She sucked her teeth. "**Nobody lyin', Wiz.**"

"**You sure?**"

"**Yes.**"

"**Aight, bet.**"

I hung up, put her address into my GPS, and made my way to her. She was gonna have to show me a clear face that wasn't streaked with tears because I wasn't convinced. It hadn't even been forty-eight hours, and shorty already had me poppin' up on her. Was this my damn soulmate?

7

ALACEA

dialed Wiz's number right back after the line went dead because I was going to give his ass a piece of my mind. I was already on ten and wasn't bout to let another nigga play with me tonight, especially a nigga that I didn't know like that. Yes, I had been crying, but that wasn't something I had to disclose to him. It was bad enough that I sat up in his car boohooing about Quan's trifling ass. The phone rang a couple times, but he didn't answer, so I sent him a text.

Me: Umm, I don't appreciate being hung up on. That shit is rude as hell. You can go on head and delete my number too.

Standing up from the couch, I went to my bedroom to run myself a bubble bath. My emotions were still very much all over the place, and even after crying earlier, I knew I had more tears in me. I'd done a good job at keeping them at bay while driving Ashlynn home. She helped by not bringing up Quan or even questioning if I'd spoken to him or not. When I got home, I had every intention to snatch every item he owned out of our shared closet, toss it in trash bags, and set them by the door, but I couldn't even make it to the bedroom. I found myself in the living room again, replaying everything in my head.

I'd seen the message that Wiz had sent and thought it was sweet that he was checking on me. Cherish had forewarned me before I left the party that he was more than likely going to ask for my number and wanted my permission to give it. I didn't mind because he'd kinda consoled me, and I honestly didn't think he'd reach out anyway. Now, I was regretting it because how dare he hang up on me with his rude ass? I had a half a mind to block him but left it alone, hoping he'd get the hint if he ever texted me again and I didn't answer.

Adding a few droplets of essential oils to my bath water, I went to strip out of my clothes when I heard my door open and close. Already knowing it was Quan, I quickly pulled my romper back over my butt and stormed out front.

"Lacey, I…" He went to speak, and I put my hand up to stop him.

"I'm good on explanations, don't have no empathy for I'm sorries, and fresh out of fucks to give when it comes to you. I hope you're here to pick up majority of your stuff."

He stood silently, and the sorry ass look on his face was pissing me off. I wanted to fight his ass, but I knew I couldn't beat him, so I wouldn't even try. I was, however, throwing bows with this nigga in my head because playing with a good heart was insane to me.

"I respect that, and I'll leave if you want me to."

"I do."

"Aight, but I just want to apologize. I didn't mean for you to find out like that. I hate that you had to find out that way forreal. I'm sorry if I embarrassed you."

"If you embarrassed me?! If?!" I shrieked. "Ain't no if. You've been embarrassing me, NayQuan. Real shit, I should be madder at myself than I am at you because you can only do to me what I allow. And I'm ashamed to say that I let so much shit slide."

"Don't cry, Alacea. I fucked up." He went to step toward me, and I stepped back, wiping the tears that I didn't even realize had fallen.

"Yes, you did. Do you have anything that you need to get right now?"

His head dropped, and he picked it back up again. "Nah."

"Okay, cool. I'll have everything packed and ready for you to grab tomorrow. Please leave."

He stared at me a few seconds, likely trying to figure out if there was anything else he could say, but he said nothing. Nodding, he turned and walked back to the door.

"Hold on. I'll take my key. When I have everything ready for you, I'll shoot you a text with a time to pick it up." I held my hand out as he took the key off the ring that he also had his car keys on. Placing it in my hand, he gave me another pitiful look. Walking past him, I went to the door and held it open, gesturing for him to leave.

"I love you, Lacey."

"Uh huh. I hope you love me enough to leave me the hell alone." As soon as he was on the other side of the door, I slammed it behind him. "Got me all the way fucked up. Moving like I ain't that girl around this bitch! The hell!" I spoke out loud to myself while marching back to my room.

Fired up, I completely disregarded the bath water and went straight for the closet. His shit had to come out asap. With each designer shirt I snatched off of the felt hangers, I felt myself more and more enraged. Once the shirts were down, I went for the sneaker boxes, tossing them out as well. I wanted to rid myself of any memory of Quan's disloyal ass. Kicking everything into a pile, I went for his dresser drawer next. Just as I went to toss his jeans, shorts, and boxers into the pile, my phone rang in the bathroom.

Stepping over the clothes, making sure to kick a couple boxes as I passed, I went to grab the phone before it stopped ringing. Recognizing the number Wiz had called from, I answered.

"It's clear that you didn't read the text I sent you." Attitude dripped from my voice, and I did nothing to hide it.

"I read it and ignored it. I need your services. I'm outside your building."

I cocked my head to the side, knowing he wasn't serious. **"Excuse me?"**

"It seems that you've talked yourself into coming to the

aid of my employee again. He busted his stitches, and I need you to take a look at it. I also need to get a look at you."

"Just who do you think you are, pulling up to my address? This is not how I do business." By now, I was so frustrated that I started pacing, and my chest was heaving up and down. Had I not glanced over at the tub, I wouldn't have noticed that my bath water was close to overflowing. **"Shit!"** I cussed while turning off the faucet.

"Ay, Beautiful, stop and take a deep breath. Come on, lemme hear you. Inhale and exhale slowly."

Tossing my head back, I wanted to fight against him but did as he instructed. Inhaling deeply, I slowly exhaled. I did it three times in succession and felt my body settle a little.

"I'll be right down."

Ending the call, I set the phone down on the counter and went to pull out a fresh pair of scrubs to change into. Grabbing my medical bag, ID, and wallet from my purse, my two phones, and a charger, I walked past Quan's stuff and toward the door. I planned to have everything packed up and waiting for him first thing in the morning. Leaving the house, I sent Lance and Blind a text, letting them know I was doing a follow-up on Wiz's people.

Brother: He already let me know.

Me: Did you give him my address?

Brother: No, Cherish did. But he let me know he was going before he got there. You know how I am about you, sis. If I felt an ounce of bullshit or questioned your safety at all, he wouldn't have made it there.

Me: Can you have Blind pick me up once I'm done? I'm not in the right headspace to drive.

Brother: Done. Text as soon as you get there and when you're ready to leave. We'll talk about your headspace in the morning.

Me: I'll text you. Love you.

I wasn't telling my brother or Blind about what went down with Quan. I'd rather pour my heart out to a stranger before I put myself through that interrogation. Taking the elevator down to the building's lobby, I pushed through the doors to find Wiz standing outside of his car, watching the street. When he saw me, he opened the passenger side door.

"Come on, Beautiful. I don't know how much longer your patient can wait."

Making my way over to him, I rolled my eyes and got in. I wasn't over him hanging up on me. "I hope you know I'm not talking to you, and I'm only doing this because I said I would."

"It's good to keep your word. It's not good to lie."

"Lie? Here you go accusing me again. Do you do that often with people you don't know?"

"Do you lie often?" he countered.

"Mann." Sucking my teeth, I went to pull the door closed, and he stopped me.

"Were you crying?"

"No, Wizdom."

"You have tear streaks on your cheeks, Beautiful." He reached out and touched my skin, sending a shiver down my spine. "Let me tell you this. If I ever see your mood shift in a sad way and I think it's about that nigga, I'ma put a hole in 'em. If I were you, I'd work on my facial expressions."

His declaration made my heart thump and clit jump. "You don't know me."

"But I want to get to know you. And in doing so, I'm liable to step on any nigga that could hinder that process. We'll talk more about it. Right now, let's get to our destination." Closing my door, he walked around to the driver's side, casually got in, and pulled off.

Cherish had warned me, and by the words he spoke, she was spot on. One part of me didn't know whether to be concerned or turned on. The other was a little bit of both.

8

WIZDOM

The drive to the trap was a quiet one until my phone rang with an incoming call from Fallon. In my haste to get to Lacey, I didn't think to let her know that I had to raincheck our fuck session. Glancing over at the back of Lacey's head as she looked out of the window, I could tell by her body language that she had a lot on her mind. It was a good thing that I couldn't see her face because I was sincere in the words I'd spoken about putting a hole in a nigga that turned her smile upside down.

"You know you don't have to ignore calls on account of me, right? You can act like I'm not even here."

I had already declined the call and sent a text to Fallon. "How long have you been doing this Emergency Service thing?"

Shifting her body in the passenger seat so that she was

81

facing me, she responded. "You know what kills me about niggas?"

"Nah, but go head and tell me."

"The fact that y'all will have a good thing at home — no, scratch that, a great thing standing right in your face — and willingly fumble it. Please enlighten me on how that shit works?" She grilled me with serious eyes, awaiting my answer.

"What do you consider a good thing?"

"What do you mean?"

"What is your definition of a good thing?"

"I'm gonna speak for myself. A good thing meaning a woman who is dedicated to you mentally and physically. A woman who puts her best foot forward to make sure you're good. Makes sure home is taken care of, whether that looks like keeping the home clean, cooking for you, and making sure I meet every sexual need. I'm a good thing."

Pulling up in front of the trap, I parked and took the keys out of the ignition. "I can only answer your question on my own behalf. I can't speak for all men cause at the end of the day, I'm me."

"Okay. Go head."

"So, if we're together and you're getting up every day to be all you can be for me and the relationship, where do you find time to be there for you?" Her brows dipped, letting me know that my question either caught her off guard or she just didn't like my response, so I elaborated. "Before you answer, understand that a man is gonna do what he wants to do whether you do all that shit you laid out or not. At the end of the day, you need to preserve self for your own peace of mind. Also, preserve yourself so when a nigga like me comes along, you're not closed off to the idea of trying again."

Dead silence filled the car for a few seconds before she spoke. "Let's go inside so I can do what I gotta do and get back home."

"Aight." I didn't push the issue because now wasn't the time. Getting out at the same time, I walked a step behind her as she entered the building. "Same door as your last visit," I directed.

Using my key, we entered the apartment, and I could hear Suge's voice from the front.

"Hold still so I can wrap this shit, man."

"Ahhh, damn, Suge. That shit hurt!" Slim's elevated voice indicated he was in pain, but I was nowhere near moved. Lacey, on the other hand, pushed forward, following their voices.

"Bout time y'all got here," Suge expressed. "Nurse Sexy, come fix this crybaby ass nigga up please. The whining shit is blowin' me."

"Ay, cut that sexy shit out. Matter fact, give her some room to work. If the count ain't finished, get on that."

Suge grinned, showing the platinum fangs in her mouth, and nodded before walking off to do what I said.

"Why can't she call me sexy?" Lacey questioned with her hand on her hip.

"Cause I said she can't," I replied simply. "Fix the man up so we can go, Beautiful."

"You bossin' me around now?"

Her stance was subtle, but the hint of flirtation was there. I took a step forward, closing the small space between us, and leaned in so that my lips were at her ear. "I'm not bossin' you around, but if that's the typa shit you like, then I can."

Cracking a slight smile, she stepped back from me and over to Slim.

"Hey, let me see what you got going on here."

I watched as she removed the bandage that Suge attempted to rewrap and assess it thoroughly. Slim grinded his teeth and took short breaths, refusing to make eye contact with me and for good reason. He knew I was gon' get on his ass about moving carelessly.

"You gotta stitch him up again?"

"Yeah."

"Damn, man," Slim let out. "You got anything stronger to numb it with? And something else for the pain after? This shit ain't no hoe."

"I'm gonna do the best I can to minimize the pain. You gotta be careful how you move around going forward though. It hasn't began healing yet."

"Aight."

A half an hour later, she'd stitched him back up, rewrapped the wound, and managed to convince me to give Slim a couple days off. The only thing that made me concede was the way she went about asking. She didn't do it in front of Slim. Instead, she pulled me to the side. The way she moved let me know that she paid attention. I didn't want him to think for a second that he was skating on his responsibilities. After giving him the clearance to head home, I made it clear that his time off would be without pay. If my pockets were hit, I had to make a nigga pay double.

"THAT WAS NICE OF YOU TO GIVE HIM THE DAYS OFF. HE'S definitely gonna need it. You can look at it as saving money too. He seems accident prone," Lacey spoke through a yawn as we sat on the couch, waiting for Blind to pick her up.

Suge had left for the night after Slim, leaving us alone. I'd offered to drive her back home, but she declined, citing that she didn't want me to have to go out of my way.

"I'm not nice, Beautiful. I'm kind. There's a difference."

"This is true. Either way, I'm sure he appreciated it."

"He won't appreciate me hitting his pockets, but hey, he gotta put his healing first, right?"

She chuckled. "Yo' sarcastic ass."

"You know we got a breakfast date in the morning, right?"

She yawned again, this time adding a stretch that made her shirt lift up a little, exposing her smooth belly. I licked my lips openly, wanting to touch her skin.

"I did agree to that, didn't I?"

"Yep, and I intend to take you out and get to know you over a good meal."

She sighed. "I'm gonna be honest with you, Wizdom. I'm fresh off of a breakup, as you can tell, and I'm really givin' a *fuck niggas* kinda vibe. I'm not sure I'll be good company right now."

Catching her sad eyes, I pulled out my phone. "What's that nigga address?"

"What nigga?"

"The nigga that broke your heart, what's his address?"

She let out a nervous laugh. "Trust me, it's not even worth it."

"Trust me, you'll feel better knowing that nigga hurtin' just like you. It'll be even worse."

"Anybody ever told you that you're crazy?"

"Yes. Along with charming and charismatic. Handsome too."

"Very," she concurred, making me smile.

"Real shit though, I'm giving you permission to use me to get over that nigga. I promise you it won't be long before you forget all about what he didn't do because you'll be so focused on what I am doing."

"Was that a sexual innuendo?"

"Hey," I threw my hands up, "if your dirty mind took you there, who am I to convince you of otherwise?"

Her phone rang, and she laughed while answering it. "**I'll be right out, cousin.**" Grabbing her medical bag, she stood, and I did the same.

"Can I hug you?"

"Ahhh, not you a *can I get a hug* ass nigga." She continued laughing, and I smiled.

"Far from it. You see how I rephrased the question."

"I peeped that. And after how you came to my rescue today, I guess a hug wouldn't be so bad."

I closed the distance between us and wrapped my arms around her. Inhaling her scent, I rubbed her back in a circular motion. The tension released from her body immediately. Had she not pulled back first, I would've held on longer.

"You good?"

She stared up at me with low eyes and nodded. "Yes," she spoke just above a whisper. "I'm okay."

I wanted to kiss her pouty lips but leaned in and kissed her forehead instead.

"You gon' be better than okay. Come on. Let me walk you out."

Walking outside, I escorted her over to Blind's car and opened the passenger side door for her to get in.

"Heard the gentleman," Blind joked from the driver's side. "Fuck outta here wit all that, Rico Suave."

Laughing, I gave him the finger as he pulled away from the curb. Once they turned the corner, I hopped in my car and sent a text to Lacey.

Me: Wear something comfortable for breakfast tomorrow, Beautiful. I just thought of somewhere else to take you after. I'll be to you by ten.

While I'd always been very forward when letting a female know that I was interested in her, it was usually on a sexual, non-committal level. With Lacey, I wanted to know more about her beyond that. This way when we did get to the sex, she'd give the pussy to me on a silver platter. I couldn't put my finger on it, but she had that thing that was worth investing my time in.

9

ALACEA

I found myself trying to hide my smile while reading Wiz's text message for the second time. He was adamant about this breakfast date that I'd agreed to under duress. When he sent the text last night, I was prepared to respond with an excuse to get out of it, but something told me to sleep on it and make my final decision in the morning. Now, here I was, standing in the middle of my closet with my phone in my hand, trying to figure out what to wear. I'd awakened earlier than I expected to with a better attitude than I had last night. Though my hurt feelings were still very fresh and raw, I made the decision to move on in peace and only leave tears for my pillow at night should I need a good cry.

As planned, I put all of Quan's belongings in trash bags and lined them up neatly at my door. Knowing that the sound of his voice would instantly trigger me, I decided not to reach out to him just yet. Finding myself indecisive about the type of comfortable look I wanted to go for, I dialed Ashlynn's number and was sent directly to voicemail. Sucking my teeth, I called Cherish next. She came through and answered on the second ring.

"Wassup, boo?"

"Hey, girl. You busy?"

"No. You need me to get dressed and put my shoes on?"

"No, crazy." I laughed. "I was calling because I need your help picking out something to wear. Is it cool to FaceTime?" Cherish wasn't the kind of person that you could just FaceTime out the blue because she always answered. Sometimes, that was a good thing, and then, other times, there was no telling what my girl could be up to, so I always confirmed beforehand.

"You know you make me sick with that, right? I'm FaceTiming you now. Pick up."

I answered the incoming video call, and she was sitting on the toilet. "This the shit I be talkin' bout. Why didn't you just say you were in the bathroom, Cherish?"

"Cause we friends, and you act like I'm on here showing you my kewchie or somethin'."

"I've seen that too."

She giggled. "I didn't show it to you, Lacey. You FaceTimed me, and I was walking around naked. There's a difference. Anyway, why you need help finding something to wear? You can dress. Where you going?"

"Out to breakfast."

"Girl, get the hell off my phone."

"What?"

"You gon' let that wack ass nigga take you out to break-fast after you just saw him at the park having family day? I know you done fell and bumped your head. You need to put your nursing degree to good use and get yo' mind right cause you are losinggg meee. Breakfast? Breakfast, Lacey?"

I shook my head at her rambling and waited for her to finish. **"You done?"**

Standing up from the toilet, she flushed it and set the phone down to where it was facing the ceiling. **"Yeah, I'm done. I'm hanging up though."**

"I'm not going out to breakfast with Quan's disloyal ass. I'm going with your brother."

The phone was back on her face in a flash, and she sported a sneaky grin. **"Oh, really? Didn't I tell you? I be knowin' what I'm talkin' about. And Wizdom don't even go after women like that. They usually flock to him."**

"It's just breakfast. Why you actin' like he asked me for my hand in marriage, girl?"

"Where y'all going to eat at?"

"I don't know. We didn't go over those details. He just said to wear something comfortable because he wanted to take me somewhere after."

"Okay, okay. Well, I apologize for jumping the gun and assuming. You in yo' *fuck that nigga* **bag, and I live, honey.**

Back to the outfit though. Ummm, you can do a little tennis skort and fitted tank combo. It's pretty hot outside, so I'd say sandals. Ooouu, make sure they have a strap. Remember, you don't know where y'all going after."

I nodded. "That sounds like a plan. Alright, thanks, girl. Let me go get myself together. He said he'll be here by ten."

"Right. You wanna be punctual on your first date."

"Shut up. It's not a date."

"So, what it is then?"

I shrugged. "An outing."

"And y'all are gonna talk and get to know each other while y'all out, right?"

"Yeah."

"Alacea, get off my phone playin' so much. Y'all going on a damn date. Have fun and call me when you get back home." She hung up on me, and I laughed at her brashness. She and Wizdom were definitely related.

I sent him a text to let him know that I was getting ready, and he responded seconds later, reminding me to dress comfortably. Tossing my phone on the bed, I hopped in the shower, looking forward to my "outing."

BREAKFAST TURNED OUT BETTER THAN I EXPECTED AND NOT just because of the food. Wizdom was good company. He'd done a good job at keeping my mind off of Quan by simply being able to hold a conversation. Not only that, but he was also funny as hell. It was clearly something that ran in his family because Cherish always had me dying laughing, even when she called herself being serious. He had jokes for everything, and my stomach was in knots from laughing so hard.

"Wiz, stoppp. They gon' put us out of this restaurant. You play too much."

"Shiiiddd, I ain't trippin' bout them puttin' us out. I'm waiting for a reason not to tip a muhfucka. I finished my chicken and waffles."

"Okay, but let me finish this pancake. Don't crack another joke please." I used my napkin to wipe the tears from my eyes.

"Aight. Go head and eat, Beautiful."

"Forreal."

"I'm forreal. Go head and eat before big foot come back over here and ask if we need anything else."

Dropping my fork, I covered my mouth to hide my giggles. "I'm done. Get the check cause you don't have no sense." As if on cue, our waiter with the extra-large feet made his way over to us, and I just knew I was gonna pee on myself.

"Can I get anything else for the two of you?"

"No," I managed to get out without snickering. "Thank you."

"Okay, here's your check whenever you're ready." He placed the black check holder in the middle of the table and went on his way.

"Fuck he think? We bout to split the bill or something?"

"You want to?" I questioned to gauge his response.

"Nah. I was thinkin' we can rock, paper, scissors this thing to see who gon' cover it all." He held his hands out, and I did the same.

"Okay, come on."

"You serious?" he questioned, slowly pulling his hands back.

"Yeah. Why not? Sounds like my typa carrying on."

"Beautiful, put yo' hands down. If that ain't some bum ass shit. Don't ever let no nigga take you on no date and try to bum his way out of paying the bill for shits and giggles."

"Okay, Boss. I won't ever let it happen again. Pinky promise." I leaned in and held up my pinky. I loved his response because I had no intentions of paying even if he accepted my offer. "Come on, lock in."

He intertwined his finger with mine, and we both nodded. "That was corny but cute. I fuck wit it."

The way we'd been smiling and laughing since arriving at the restaurant, one would think we were the happiest couple.

"Where we going after this?"

"Can't tell you that, Beautiful. You just gotta roll wit me on the strength. We're actually going two places, and I think you'll appreciate the thought I put into them both."

I was anxious to know what he had in store but remained patient and didn't inquire further. "Okay. I'll let you take the lead today."

"That position suits me well. What position works for you?"

My mind navigated to a dirty place that I didn't bother to steer in the right direction. "I happen to have expertise in all of them actually."

Licking his lips, he showed his pearly whites. "Say dat then. Let's get outta here. Before we head to the first place, we gotta get you changed out of those sandals and into some sneakers."

"Sneakers? I like my sandals." I glanced down at my Valentino thong sandals while exiting the booth.

"Me too. You have pretty feet. Where we're going requires sneakers though."

"I can just run home and change."

"Ay, this my date. Let me do me. You can make plans on the next one."

I wanted to refute the whole date thing, but I let it go because I was really having a good time so far. "Okay. You got it."

He dropped a couple twenties on the table and held out his hand for me to grab. I did, and surprisingly, it didn't feel weird or forced. He made it feel natural by not pausing awkwardly to see my response. We just kept moving out of the restaurant and to his car.

"There's a sneaker store two blocks from here. You wanna walk or take the car?"

The sun was out, but the heat wasn't unbearable, so I opted to walk. "You gonna hold my hand the whole time?"

"Yeah. And you gotta walk on the inside of the street, Beautiful. What kinda niggas you been fuckin' wit?" He switched places with me, and we began walking.

"Apparently the wrong ones. Does Fallon walk on the inside of the street when y'all go out too?"

"It's rare that we go out. But when we do, yeah, I make sure she's on the inside. Just like I make sure she never pulls out her wallet if we go anywhere. Is that your way of asking wassup with the two of us?"

"Is that your way of answering?" I countered.

"Me and Fallon aren't a couple. I wouldn't call what we do dating either. We fuck wit each other though. I don't have any rights to her, and she doesn't have any to me."

"In other words, y'all just fuck and enjoy each other's company from time to time?"

"Basically."

"Okay." I appreciated his honesty and didn't feel the need to elaborate on the topic any further.

"What size shoe you wear?" he asked as we entered Foot Locker.

"I'm a six in boys. Eight in women."

"Aight. Pick out what you want."

"Oh, I have a say so? I thought this was your date."

"Touché. You sit down, and I'ma get you right."

I went to sit down and felt a pair of eyes on me. Turning my head, I spotted Quan in the infant sneaker section, burning a hole in my face with his stare. Unlike the look of surprise he had at the park, his eyes were narrow and menacing, letting me know that it was likely that he saw me and Wiz enter the store. Just as I went to look away, the same female from the park walked up to him with their baby strapped to her chest and hit his arm to get his attention. Standing, I walked over to where Wiz stood, talking to one of the sales associates, and locked my arm in his.

"You like these?" He held up a pair of gold and white ASICS Gel 1130s.

"Yeah. I have 'em in navy blue."

"Cool. Can we get these in a size eight?"

The associate nodded and walked off to get the shoe. I felt my mood shifting and did my best to shake it, but my best was failing me. Angling my body so that I was standing in front of him, I blinked back tears.

"Talk to me," he encouraged, placing his hand on the back of my neck and massaging it.

It eased my tension a little but not enough. "My ex is here with his baby and the baby's mom. I'm about to cry, and I don't want to. I also don't want you feeling like you need to do anything on account of me."

"You still want him?"

I paused, choosing my words wisely. "No, but..."

"Cool. Come on." Taking my hand in his, he guided me toward the exit, and we walked back to his car in silence.

As he started up the car, I reached out and touched his arm. "Hey, I know you had this day planned out, but if you don't mind, can you just take me home? I really enjoyed breakfast, but my mind is not all the way there, and I'd hate to be bad company after you put thought into the day."

"I respect that. Another day, another time?" He held his pinky up. "This is our thing now."

"Another day, another time." I did the same, holding my pinky up to lock with his.

I didn't know when that day and time would be, but I had a feeling that he wouldn't be too far for me to reach.

WIZDOM

"**G**oddamn, Fallon. You eatin' that dick up like you miss a nigga or somethin'."

I looked down into Fallon's brown eyes as she kneeled before me with her face in my lap. She'd been in that position for the last ten minutes, refusing to let me go. *Gawk, gawk, gawk.* The sounds of her gaggin' filled my bedroom as she sucked me up like her life depended on it. I guess not seeing me for two weeks had her wanting to make up for lost time.

Slowly pulling my dick from her mouth, she slapped it against her lips. "You like that, Daddy?"

"Fuckkk, yeah." I thrusted upward as she jerked my dick with one hand and used the other to play with my balls.

"I missed you so much. Can you put that big dick inside of me and make ya nasty bitch cum?"

Fallon had no inhibitions when we fucked and often let me slut her out to my satisfaction. Knowing that she was this kind of freak with me and we weren't exclusive, I could only imagine how far she went with whoever else she was fuckin'. Let her tell it, she was locked in with me only. I wasn't a fool by a long shot. She didn't have to cap me down. I just enjoyed her when we were together and didn't give any thought to what she did when we weren't.

"Grab a rubber and put it on," I instructed with my dick still standing at attention.

She happily obliged, standing in all her nakedness and reaching into my nightstand to grab a condom. Ripping the package open with her teeth, she went to slide it on me but was interrupted by the front door alarm going off.

"Wizdom!" I heard Cherish yell out my name, and Fallon's face went from passion filled to sour. The transition made me laugh inwardly. Fallon knew that my sister wasn't a fan of hers, and Cherish didn't try to hide it. "Wizdom!" she called out again.

Standing from the edge of the bed, I picked up my basketball shorts from the floor and threw them on along with a t-shirt. "Gimmie a minute," I said to Fallon.

"Really, Wizdom? I'm standing here naked with a wet pussy. You can't wait to talk to your sister?"

"You can wait here, or you can get dressed, Fallon. I ain't trippin.'" I hadn't gotten my shit off yet, but it wasn't nothing that my hand and some Vaseline couldn't take care of.

She scoffed and plopped down on the bed. "Don't take all

day, Daddy. She needs you." Spreading her legs to give me an eyeful of her bald pussy, she stuck her tongue out at me.

As tempting as it was to dive headfirst into her wet box, I knew the level of ignorant Cherish could get to. It was too late to be up refereeing a fight that Fallon was sure to lose. "Keep it wet."

Leaving the room, I made sure to close the door behind me. As I made my way to the front of my place, Cherish was on her way to the back.

"You got me yellin' through the house like a crazy person. What you was doing?"

"Bout to bust a nut till you came through yellin' like a crazy person. Wassup?"

"Ewww. I ain't need to know all that."

"Shit, you asked. What you want, and why you keep poppin' up unannounced?" I walked past her to guide her back to the front.

"I can't check on my brother now?"

"Bam, don't bullshit me. You don't pop up late at night. You fightin' witcho bum? I need to put my shit on?"

"No. And stop callin' him that 'fore I go in the room and beat yo' prostitute up. When the last time you spoke to Lacey?" Sitting her purse and keys down on the kitchen island, she washed her hands and went into the fridge. Grabbing a bag of grapes, she hopped up on the counter.

"I sent her a text this morning. Why? She aight?"

I hadn't seen Lacey since the day she cut our date short. That didn't stop me from sending her texts here and there.

I'd even sent flowers a few times with little notes and shit reminding her to smile. Every note would end with me requesting to see a picture of her face after she received the flowers. I'd received eight pictures so far, and each one had a genuine smile, so I assumed she was good.

"Yeah. I think you should go see her."

Leaning back against the counter, I folded my arms across my chest. "Oh, now you tryna put me on to your friend?"

She shrugged. "I figured since she said y'all had a good time on the first date, why not take her on a few more? We can't risk her doubling back to Quan."

I went to respond and heard footsteps coming toward us. Fallon rounded the corner, dressed in one of my t-shirts. The shirt barely covered her ass, causing Cherish's face to frown up as she walked past.

"Scuse me. Sorry to interrupt. I just wanted to grab something to drink." Fallon sauntered over to me and opened the fridge.

"Anyway, are you gonna go see her?" Cherish questioned.

"Yeah. I am. Ay, you got what you need?" I asked Fallon who still had the refrigerator door open, staring at the shelves.

"Right," Cherish added. "She actin' like you got a variety of shit in there. Like girl, grab a water or a juice and go."

"Chill, Bam."

Closing the fridge, Fallon cut her eyes at Cherish before leaving the kitchen emptyhanded.

"Yeah. You need to stop wasting time with her. She don't bring shit to the table but a pretty face, that's a seven at best, and a pussy. There's plenty of that out here. You need a woman who don't care about status, got her shit together, and who you can bring home to Mommy."

I smirked. "Fallon met Mommy."

Grabbing a handful of grapes from the bag, she hopped down off the counter and picked up her purse. "Yeah, and she didn't have nothing nice to say. Neither did Aunt Dotty."

"Aunt Dotty ain't never got nothing nice to say."

"True. But I concur with her assessment of ol' girl. I'ma get outta here though. The petty part of me is just itching to hurt a bitch feelings. Go see my girl."

"Good night, sis. I love you. Call me when you get home."

"I will. Love you too and do the right thing. And open a window. It smell like fried fish in here." She made sure to say her last statement out loud, sticking her tongue out as she left.

Shaking my head, I laughed because she knew just like I did that Fallon was listening. Returning to my bedroom, I found Fallon sitting on the bed, fully dressed with her legs tightly crossed.

"Who am I, Wiz?"

Leaning against the door frame, I answered her question with a smile. "You're Fallon."

"Don't play wit me please."

"Nah, you don't play witchu. What you wanna ask me, Fallon?"

"Who am I to you? Like what are we doing?"

Not one to beat around the bush, I gave a simple answer to her simple question. "You are Fallon to me. We chill, fuck, and enjoy each other's company."

"And you don't see more?"

"I don't and neither do you."

Her mouth dropped. "Wow. You not gon' sugarcoat it or nothin'?"

"I ain't been doing that, won't start tonight."

"Welp, I guess I'll go since you have somewhere to be anyway, right?"

"And by how quickly you got dressed, I'm sure you do too. See, we know what this is. Let me walk you out." I started to address the ear hustling, but I knew it would be my last encounter with Fallon. "Be good, shorty."

"Uh huh, you too."

I watched as she stepped inside the elevator, and once the doors closed, I sent Lacey a text.

Me: Beautiful, you up?

Lacey: No. Lol.

Me: Well, get up. I wanna see you.

A FaceTime call came through from her, and I declined it.

Lacey: You must not wanna see me that bad.

Me: 😊 I do. But I wanna see you in person. I had it in mind to just show up at your crib, but I wanna do things different.

Lacey: You decided that the unhinged way wasn't the way to go, huh?

Me: Lol. Not tonight.

Lacey: I guess you can stop by for a few. Have you eaten?

Realizing that I hadn't eaten since earlier in the day, my stomach growled at her mentioning food.

Me: Nah, I haven't. I can stop and pick something up on the way. What you in the mood for?

While waiting for her to respond, I changed out of my basketball shorts. I put on a pair of boxers and some sweat shorts. Grabbing my keys, wallet, and gun from the nightstand, I made my way out the door.

Lacey: Sorry for the delayed response. You don't have to pick up anything. I cooked. Do you like BBQ chicken?

Me: Hell yeah. With some yellow rice and broccoli with cheese. Fuck the whole meal up.

Lacey: That's crazy. That's the exact meal I made.

Me: Damn, Beautiful. I'm tryna give you space to be single, but you making this shit hard.

Lacey: 😇 Boy, let me know when you're five minutes away, so I can heat the food up.

Me: Aight, bet. Oh, and don't try to get all cute for a nigga either. I wanna see you in your element when you're just lounging around the crib. Leave the lashes on the bathroom counter.

Lacey: See you when you get here. Bye, Wizdom.

Starting up my car, I sent a message to Suge that I was not to be disturbed unless it was an emergency. Lacey would have all of my attention tonight.

～

"Damn, girl. You might can burn. It smells good in here." Whatever she had seasoned her chicken with could be smelled at the door as she held it open for me.

"Oh, I know I can get down in the kitchen," she complimented herself. "Come in. Do you mind taking your shoes off?"

"It's your crib, Beautiful. I'll take whatever you want me to take off."

Giving me a sneaky smile, she shook her head. "You just got here and starting up already. Go wash your hands so you can eat. I set you up at the table unless you wanna eat in the living room."

I discreetly scanned her spot and nodded in satisfaction. It didn't show any signs of a male presence, and I was pleased with that. The place mirrored her chill aura and felt homely.

"I'll eat it in the kitchen or the living room." After not getting off with Fallon before leaving the house, seeing Lacey's thick thighs in a pair of pajama shorts and the way her titties sat up in her tank top had my dick semi hard.

"You go to the bathroom down the hall. First door on your right. I'm gonna go put on some pants. I can already see your wandering eyes."

"Oh, a nigga damn sure lookin'." We turned at the same time to go in the opposite direction, only I glanced back after a few steps to get a look at that ass from behind in the shorts. "I just know that pussy fat," I said out loud.

"I heard you, Wizdom. Go wash your hands!"

I laughed at her scolding and went to do as she instructed. Again, I looked around. There was nothing like a neat female, and from what I could tell, Lacey kept her place organized, clean, and it smelled good. My mama always said that if a person didn't have a clean kitchen and bathroom, then I better make damn sure I didn't eat out of their house. Using the paper towels she had on the sink to dry my hands after washing, I went to throw it away and caught a glimpse of a First Response pregnancy test in the trash. The way it was placed, I was unable to get a look at the results due to the tissue that was wrapped around part of the testing applicator.

I found myself wondering if it was positive or not. I'd made my interest clear, and while her being pregnant wouldn't turn me away, how she planned to go about the situation as far as the father was concerned could. Dropping the paper towel in the trash, I exited the bathroom and found her sitting at the table with a bottle of wine and a plate that had a hefty amount of food on it that I assumed was for me.

"What can I get you to drink?"

"I'll take any kind of juice you have," I replied, sitting down across from her.

"Tropicana Island Punch okay?"

"Yeah."

She stood, and I noticed that she had changed out of her pajama shorts and into a pair of pajama pants. They did nothing to hide all that ass she had, but I didn't comment on it, just enjoyed the view in silence.

"Here you go." She placed the glass of juice in front of me and sat back down.

"You wanna say grace?"

Her face showed confusion. "Umm, yeah. We can."

"What? You don't believe in God?"

"No, crazy. I mean, I do. I guess I just didn't expect you to wanna say grace."

"Oh, well, yeah. Gotta thank the big man upstairs. I pray over everything I eat." I winked, and she pulled at my hand before squeezing it.

"God, forgive this man for coming before you with impure thoughts in advance."

Chuckling, I grabbed her other hand, closed my eyes, and said a quick prayer over the food.

"Amen," we said in unison.

"I like your spot."

"Thank you. It's my peaceful sanctuary."

I took a bite of the chicken and licked my lips, instantly loving the sweet and savory sauce. "This honey barbeque?"

"Yeah. Straight from scratch. We don't do the jar over here," she stated matter of factly with a twist of her neck.

"You've checked another box, Beautiful. If you keep it up, I'ma have to ask who sent you."

She grinned shyly. "Who sent me?"

"Yeah. Who sent you and why?" Placing a forkful of the broccoli and rice in my mouth, I gave her a thumbs up.

"Glad you like it. How was your day?"

"It was smooth. Did some running around earlier and played the crib the rest of the day."

"How's my patient doing?"

"He straight. How are you?"

"You know you've asked me that every day for the past two weeks, right?"

I nodded and chewed, thinking about the pregnancy test in the bathroom. "Yeah. And I've been letting you slide with the *I'm good, Wizdom.* Now that we're face to face, I can see if that's true."

Leaning back in her chair, she shifted her eyes from mine to the wine bottle and from the wine bottle back up to me. I continued to eat, not wanting to force her to speak if she wasn't sure of what she wanted to say.

"I took a pregnancy test," she finally let out after a few minutes of silence.

"Word?"

"Yeah. I'll admit, the first couple days you asked me how I was doing, I wasn't good. I didn't wanna speak life into those words by saying it out loud though. Then my body started to feel off. I took it as side effects of the breakup and figured it would pass after a few days. Then, two weeks went by, and I still felt off, so on a whim, I went and bought the pregnancy test. I don't know why I'm telling you this."

"What the test say?"

She dropped her head, making me sit up straight in my seat. Lifting her head slowly, she revealed a wide grin.

"It was negative."

"Come on now, Beautiful. You had a nigga over here nervous."

She giggled. "Why?"

"Uhh, if you haven't noticed already, I'm tryna see wassup witchu."

"Still?" Her voice increased in pitch.

"Yeah, girl. You think gangstas just send flowers, notes, and good morning texts on the strength?"

She giggled, shaking her head. "I don't know what gangstas do, Wizdom. I love the flower arrangements though, and every note was thoughtful. You've managed to keep a smile on my face without being overbearing."

"That was the goal." Finishing my last bite, I downed the glass of juice and stood to stretch. "You did your thing, Beautiful."

"So, what if I was pregnant?"

"I would've helped you raise a young king. Can I take this to the kitchen?"

"No. I got it. And you've already made your interest in me clear. You don't have to go just saying stuff to get your foot in the door." Picking up my plate and glass, she went to walk to the kitchen, and I stopped her.

"Alacea," I called her by her government, "I'm a grown ass man that ain't gotta cap to get in good with a soul. I'm attracted to you and want the chance to get to know you exclusively. Had your test been positive, it wouldn't have changed that because my mind was already made up from the door that I was gonna pursue you. I get the skepticism though because the reality is we don't know each other, but that's why people date, right?"

"I guess when you put it like that, you're right," she replied.

"Cool. You can go head and tell dude from the park it's a wrap. All communication must cease. Won't nothing good come out of him tryna double back with me in the picture now."

"Does that go for Fallon too? Cause you can't exclusively date me and think you gon' fuck on her. Been there, done that, never doin it again." Her tone was firm and unwavering. I couldn't help but to lean in and kiss her full lips.

"I plan to be too busy fuckin' on you to worry bout fuckin' on anybody else, Beautiful. I'll help you wash the dishes and put the food away."

In all my twenty-eight years of living, I'd never dated anyone exclusively, but Lacey seemed worth giving it a try. She needed to be put onto some real shit, and I was the realest, so she was in good hands.

11

ALACEA

I'd experienced a rollercoaster of emotions over the last two weeks, and it was safe to say that I was able to shake back from my breakup with Quan. Seeing him out with his family again not even a full twenty-four hours later really solidified things for me. And immediately after Wiz dropped me off home, I called Quan to collect his things. I made sure to leave the bags in the hallway to avoid any interaction with him. It was a good thing that he came and left without incident because had he come on bullshit, I would've had no choice but to get my brother involved.

Bittersweet relief washed over me as his exit marked an end to what once was and would no longer be. Moving on from Quan wasn't just about removing his presence from my life but reclaiming time I'd wasted being committed to someone who clearly didn't value me. As the days passed, I went through a range of emotions, and I felt them both mentally and physically. That physical part started to become a little strange around day six when I realized that my period was three days late. A late period was a rarity for me, so just to ease my mind, I took a test.

Thankfully, it was negative. I didn't want any attachments to Quan moving forward. The one bright side through my breakup had surprisingly been Wizdom. I thought for sure that after ending our date, he was going to write me off, but he did the exact opposite. He offered his support in the most thoughtful ways that kept me smiling through tears. Every day, without fail, I received a flower delivery with a note attached. Each note was more encouraging than the last, making me blush and laugh at his attempts to be poetic but still keep it gangsta.

One in particular read, **"Beautiful, remember when you're the prize, it's never a loss. Fuck wit me and let a real nigga show you the meaning of reciprocity."**

It was so sweet mixed with a little hood, and I loved it. So much so, I called Ashlynn and read it to her. She encouraged me to take him up on his offer, and that said a lot. I wondered if her push had anything to do with her little not so secret thing she'd started with his brother.

"A dollar for your thoughts," Wiz uttered from behind me where he stood watching as I cleared my dishwasher.

Turning to face him, I used my hip to close the dishwasher and leaned back against it. "I thought it was a penny for your thoughts?"

"It is. But I ain't no cheap nigga, and what if you have a lot to say?"

I laughed at his thought process. "You just be saying shit."

"I be making sense though. Ay, let's play a game."

"Okay."

"Aight. We gon' start out with two truths and a lie. We each gotta figure out the lie."

"Okay. Ummm, I'm adopted, I used to steal lip gloss out of the beauty supply store, and I want two sets of twins." I kept my face straight to avoid giving away which statement may have been the lie.

Stroking his beard, he locked eyes with me, and I almost smiled. Wiz was so damn handsome.

"Before I answer, let's make this more interesting. For every answer we get wrong, we take a shot."

I let the idea swim around in my head for a minute and thought what the hell. I was already home, so if I got drunk, I could pass out on my couch. "Okay. White or dark?"

"White. That brown bring out the dog in me. Fuck around and have you bent over the sink, slow stroking you to oblivion."

Crossing one leg over the other, I felt myself getting horny at his admission. Opting out of responding, I reached down into my liquor cabinet. Grabbing a bottle of Don Julio 1942, I sat it down on the counter along with two shot glasses.

"I guess we're gonna test your control. Which one is the lie?"

"You were adopted."

"Nope. That's a fact. Take a shot, love. Here." I held out the bottle for him. "I'll let you pour your own troubles."

"You were adopted?"

"Yep."

Curiosity was written all over his face as he threw the shot back. "So, Lance isn't your biological brother?"

"No. But never let him hear you say it. That shit pisses him off. Can't nobody tell him that I'm not his baby sis." I beamed thinking about how protective my brother was over me.

"Respect."

"You wanna ask more questions, don't you?"

"Not if you'd rather not answer."

"It's cool. I'll give you the summarized version. I was adopted by my godparents when I was one after my mother died in a house fire. My biological mother and Lance's mother had been best friends since teenagers, and she had it written in her will that if anything were to ever happen to her, I was to be left in her care. She had adoption papers already drawn up and everything. So, yeah, that's about it."

"Were you in the house when it happened?"

"No. It was a dope house… my mother's dope house."

"Word?"

"Uh huh. I learned later in life that my mother was one of the females in Harlem getting to it in the 70s."

"You miss her?"

"Everyday. But don't make me sad. It's your turn." I'd had

two glasses of wine prior to his arrival, and it didn't take much for me to get emotional. As far as I was concerned, Wizdom had seen enough of my tears.

"I've been engaged, I'm claustrophobic, I have a Master's in Business Management." His lips formed a straight line, and I already knew what the lie was.

"Okay, number one is definitely a boldface lie." I waited for him to refute my claim, and he said nothing, making my jaw drop. "What?? You've been engaged?"

"Man, hell naw." He cracked up laughing.

"Wizdom, really?" Laughing along with him, I slapped his arm.

"I ain't never had a woman to be engaged to, girl."

"Now, that's sad. Come on, my turn."

By the time we finished the game, I'd had four shots to his two, and just as I was at my tipsy point, the sexual questions began.

"When's the last time you had that pussy kissed, Beautiful?"

Sucking my bottom lip into my mouth, I crossed my legs tightly. The last time I had sex with Quan was a couple weeks ago, and I was long overdue for some good dick.

"Why?"

"Cause I wanna put you up on this counter and suck the juices out yo' panties before I suck em' outta you."

I cracked a lazy smile. "Is that the liquor talkin'?"

"I could blame it on the liquor, but nah, this all me."

"Did you come over with the intentions to fuck?"

"Nah, but I'm not against it."

"I got another game. Whoever cum first gotta pay the other person's rent next month."

Pushing off of the counter, he stepped forward and pulled me to him by the hem of my shirt. "Go head and Zelle me now, Beautiful. I'm bout to make that pussy cream."

"Pinky swear?" I licked my lips and held up my pinky.

"Pinky swear." Linking our fingers, he leaned in and kissed my lips.

I deepened the kiss, parting his lips with my tongue. I was so turned on that I took the lead and tugged at his shorts. Catching my drift, he untied them, giving me access to his dick. Feeling the girth of his veiny piece in my hand, I stroked it softly until he fully came alive. Tearing my lips away from his, I pushed him back a little to give myself room to squat before him. Pulling his shorts down so that they rested at his ankles, I salivated. His dick was a shade darker than his skin complexion but nothing short of circumcised perfection. Sticking my tongue out, I licked from the base all the way up to the thick, mushroom tip.

"Mmmm," he uttered a low moan.

"$3,275," I let out in a seductive whisper before swallowing as much of his dick as my small mouth could take.

"Shittt, girllll." He threw his head back and rested his hand on the back of my head. "I'll have it for you in the morning. Suck that dick just like that."

The seat of my panties were soaked at his encouragement. There was something about having a man powerless under my tongue that excited me. I continued to suck him up at a rapid pace, alternating from one hand assistance to two hands. Spit slid out the sides of my mouth and down my cheeks, and I watched excitedly as his face contorted, and he pumped in and out of my mouth.

"Ya mouth so warm, Beautiful. You look so fucking good on your knees with this dick in there. So fucking beautiful." He complimented me sweetly while slowly easing his dick to the back of my throat. "There we go right there. Oooh, shit, you gon' make me bust."

My eyes watered, and I felt my gag reflexes tapping in, but I still held on like a big girl. Knowing that a nigga loved to see you near death when sucking him, I twisted my neck in a circular motion twice, and he gripped my shoulder with his free hand and pulled his dick out with the other, releasing on my marble floors.

"Ahhhh, ahhhh, fuckkk."

I looked on in amazement as the cum leaked out of his dick. It looked different — healthy. I waited until he regained his composure to stand up straight.

"You straight?" I mimicked him, and he chuckled.

"Yeah, I'm straight, but you bout to be walking funny. Where yo room at?"

"Follow me." I walked past him, leaving a trail of my clothes as I stripped out of them.

I'd done my part of getting Quan out of my system by ridding my house of him; now, I was gonna let Wiz fill every hole, thus closing a chapter and beginning a new story.

12

WIZDOM

The sunlight sliced through the gap in Lacey's sheer curtains, marking the seventh new day that I'd awakened with her asleep next to me peacefully. Watching her chest rise and fall, my mind drifted to last night. It was another night of toe-curling sex and getting to know each other. Since the first night that she let me between her legs, I'd only left her crib to grab clothes from my place. It marked the first time ever that I was able to fall back from the streets and delegate from afar. And it wasn't at her request as she didn't demand my time. Being around Lacey felt like a vacation without having to leave the crib.

Over the last few days, we'd spent time asking thought provoking questions and giving our take on relationships, both platonic and romantic. It was a change of pace from just fucking and going on my way immediately after. It was something I could see me dedicating myself to.

"Morning," she murmured, her voice still heavy with sleep.

"Morning, Beautiful," I replied, sitting up with my back against the headboard. "You slept alright?"

"I slept great," she said with a small smile tugging at her lips. She'd been doing that a lot without encouragement lately. "How'd you sleep?"

She turned so that she was laying on her side, making the sheet that covered her fall, exposing her perfect titties. She had the prettiest areoles I'd ever seen. They were dark brown in hue and slightly larger than the ones I'd seen but perfect.

"I've slept better over the past couple days than I have in the last year," I admitted.

"Not used to having a body next to you, huh? That smooth leg over yours in the middle of the night hit different."

Chuckling, I nodded. "It do. You have any plans for today? I was thinkin' we could continue the first date we never really finished."

"No plans. Surprisingly, your sister and my cousin haven't reached out to me to drag me out of the house for girls' night. They done forgot about me."

"I don't think so. Bam know you wit me, so that's probably why she hasn't reached out. And I'm sure my brother somewhere doing what we been doing the last couple nights with your cousin. I taught him well. A few pumps to the left and a swirl. Stroke 101."

"You stupid." She threw a pillow at me before standing up and going into the bathroom.

"Pussy just sittin' up early in the morning, damn."

"Shut up, nasty!" she yelled out, closing the bathroom door.

My phone buzzed on the nightstand, and I looked over at the screen to see my mother calling. Picking up the phone, I answered.

"Wassup, Ma?"

"Hey, son. What you up to?"

"Just getting up for the day. What you doin'?"

"Cooking. Felt like making brunch today. You should come over. Keem and Bam headed this way in a few."

Thinking about my date with Lacey, I hesitated for a minute before answering. I wondered if she'd be up for brunch with the fam.

"Uhhh, yeah, Ma. I'll slide through. I'm bringing a plus one."

"To who house? Mine? I know hell done froze over. Is it the girl from Dooty's party?" she asked, her tone dripping with curiosity.

"You'll see when I get there," I replied, chuckling.

She laughed. **"Alright then. I'll see you when you get here. It's ten now, try to make it before twelve."**

"Aight, Ma. I love you."

"I love you too."

I hung up, and Lacey reentered the room in a robe.

"Had to brush my teeth to give you a proper good morning," she said, climbing back in the bed.

"Shitt, you bout to open the back of that good throat up?" I pulled the sheet off me, and my dick spring up.

Her head fell back, and she laughed out loud. "No, Wizdom. A kiss, nasty."

"Oh, I didn't brush my teeth yet."

"No tongue then." She leaned over and poked her lips out.

Giving her two quick pecks, I pulled her up so that her head was on my shoulder. "So, umm, change of plans," I said, scratching the back of my head. "How you feel about coming with me to my mom's house for brunch?"

She looked up at me with raised brows. "Brunch at your mother's house? I don't know, Wiz. I mean, I've met your mom before and love her down but..."

"I get that. But it's nothing serious. Just brunch. Some good food and family vibes. No pressure. Trust me, I'm not gonna get down on one knee."

She chewed on her bottom lip, thinking it over. "Okay, I can do brunch. And you have to behave, Wizdom."

"Girl, this my mama house we going to. I know how to act."

"Mmhmm."

"Come get in the shower with me so I can fuck you up against the wall before we leave. She wants me there before twelve."

"See," she pointed her finger at me, getting out of the bed, "that's what I'm talkin' bout."

"Oh, you don't want me to be myself? This me, Beautiful. I talk nasty. I'll tone it down when we get there though. Pinky promise." Locking pinkies to seal it, we hopped in the shower. "Go head and touch ya toes for me," I whispered in her ear, sinking my teeth in her neck and giving it a light suck.

"Sssssss, Wizdom," she hissed, bending over.

I took a moment to rub her booty before giving it a hard slap that could be heard throughout the bathroom. After sex the first time, she assured me that she was on birth control and wasn't looking to have kids any time soon, giving me free rein to spray paint her walls. Sliding into her slowly, until my dick had reached the hilt of her pussy, I rested there for a moment to relish in her wetness.

"Throw that shit back like I like it, Beautiful. We don't have long so go head and get that nut, so I can go flaunt you around the family."

PULLING UP TO MY MOTHER'S HOUSE IN JERSEY, I SPOTTED both Cherish and Keem's cars in her driveway. Neither had texted me to see if I was coming, so I figured my mother didn't mention it either.

"Cherish is here too?"

"Yeah. You cool with that?"

"Of course. I miss my friend, and I don't have to smother you."

"You mean the opposite way around. Yo' ass scared I'ma grab ya titty in front of my mama or something."

"Omg, you betta not."

"Relax, Beautiful. I'll be on my best behavior. Plus, my brother here, so I'ma chop it up with him, so you can spend some time with your homegirl before I get back to holding you hostage."

She smiled genuinely. "Aww, you like hanging with lil' ol' me?"

"Yeah. You got this thing about you that settles me. It's weird, but I fuck wit it."

Unbuckling her seatbelt, she leaned over and kissed my lips. "And here I was thinkin' it was this good snatcha watcha."

"Icing on the cake, Beautiful."

She puckered her lips to kiss me again, this time feeding me her tongue. She let out a soft moan that made my dick rise in my shorts. I went to grab the back of her neck, only to be stopped by a knock at my window.

Lacey giggled, wiping her lip gloss from my lips. "Look." She pointed behind me, and I turned to see my sister and her cousin standing at the window with their arms crossed, mugging.

"Let her out the car, Wizdom," Cherish spoke up, pulling at my door handle. "You had her all week."

"Lemme get out before they jump you."

"Yeah, you do that cause you was one moan away from getting fucked right in this car."

She quickly opened the door and scurried out. The trio embraced each other and walked hand in hand up the driveway.

"Y'all some haters!" I yelled out to them as they entered the house at the same time Keem walked out.

I watched as he exchanged a few words with Ashlynn that had her blushing before he kissed her neck and bopped over to my car.

"She done put that shit on you," I teased as he hopped in my passenger seat.

"Nigga, in the worst way." He dapped me up, laughing. "C'mon, we gotta make a supermarket run for Mommy."

"How I get caught up on an errand she sent you on, bro?"

"Man, you wanna ride with me or sit in there with the women and listen to them talk about us?"

Starting up the car, I reversed out of the driveway. "I ain't gon' argue witchu there, my boy." I knew I didn't want any parts of that conversation. "Wassup though? I ain't heard much from you since the party."

"Ain't shit. Working, taking care of that bad ass nephew of yours, and most recently, getting to know Ashlynn."

"That's wassup. So far so good?"

"Shit, she bout to be y'all sister-in-law and don't even know it. Bro, she is the female me, even down to the way she deal with her son pops. I done already threatened this girl while I was in the pussy. That's how lethal that shit is. Wait, remind me to never say that shit again. I can't be out here discussing my girl pussy witchu."

"Respect. I ain't plan on tellin' you shit bout Lacey's." Just thinkin' about the way her walls squeezed me like the warmest hug when I was between her legs made me lick my lips.

"You think she the one?"

"She something special fa sho."

"Bam told Mommy she the one."

"Yo sister so nosey, dawg."

"She is. You know Mommy set this whole thing up on purpose, right?"

Pulling into the parking lot of the supermarket, I turned the car off.

"For what?"

"She wanted to see how you interacted with Alacea. Said she ain't never known you to be boo'd up with nobody, so she had to see it for herself."

"She ain't even know I was bringing her."

He chuckled. "Man, this **our** mama you talkin' bout, and Bam is our sister. You think she ain't tell her who you was wit?"

"Nosey as hell. Go head and get what you came for so we can head back."

"Aight."

While waiting for him, I checked on Lacey.

Me: Whatever they saying, confirm it with me first, Beautiful. Until you confirm it, I plead the fifth.

Lacey: lol how you know we even discussing you?

Me: Trust me, I know.

Lacey: Your mom seems to think you like me. Say she knew there was nothing going on with Fallon when she watched you chase me in the park and pick me up. You was dead wrong for that lol.

Me: I know. Fallon told me that day.

Lacey: Where'd you go?

Me: I'm at the store with Keem. You miss me already?

Lacey: Yes.

Me: I'm on my way back.

"Mommy might be on to something," I said to Keem as he entered the car.

Things between Lacey and I were quickly unfolding like a blank canvas. Today was just brunch with the fam, but it felt like the first real step toward something more. Time would tell where it would lead.

ALACEA

"Look at her over there texting and smiling and shit."

I glanced up from my phone and stuck my tongue out at Ashlynn, sliding it back into my purse. "Ain't nobody blushing. Y'all missed me?"

As soon as we'd entered the house, they dragged me to the backyard and put a mimosa in my hand.

"You don't fuck wit us," Ash continued with a playful roll of her eyes.

"Nah, y'all don't fuck wit me," Cherish chimed in. "Y'all done got with my brothers and said forget Cherish." Taking a sip of her mimosa, she shook her head.

"Bitch, please. You only called me once in the last week," Ash said, laughing.

"And ain't called me not once, tuh." I added.

"Well, yo ass," she pointed to Ash, "only answered once and let Keem ugly ass hang up on me. And I ain't call Lacey cause Wiz sent me a text talkin' bout in order to get to know you, he need your undivided attention. Getting on my nerves already."

"I have a confession to make," Ash proclaimed with her finger raised. "It was me that hung up on you when you called, friend."

"Ooouu, you so trifling!" Cherish exclaimed.

"I'm sorry, boo. Yo' brother got this thing that he do with his..."

"Bitch, you betta not," Cherish warned, and I burst out laughing.

"Y'all come inside, so we can eat. The boys are back," her mother announced.

"Y'all lucky y'all don't have no brothers I wanna fuck on cause oouuu, I would make y'all feel it."

I threw my arms around her neck and kissed her cheek with Ash doing the same to the other side.

"You happy for us, ain't you?"

"Yeah, I guess if y'all gon' be with anyone, it may as well be some real ones. But I wanna say this to you, Lacey." I let her neck go, and she grabbed both of my hands. "Brother or not, if you feel shit start going left and like that nigga ain't valuing you like the custom ass bitch you are, LEAVE. Ain't no nigga worth you going through what you went through with whatshisname. You deserve the moon, the stars, and the fuckin' planets too. We know that, you know that, and Wizdom clearly sees that. Move accordingly."

I teared up as we embraced each other.

"You betta not be out here cryin', Beautiful." I heard Wizdom's voice and shook my head.

"Shut up, Wizdom!" Cherish yelled out to him. "Girl, wipe yo face before he see you. I don't wanna hear his mouth."

"Me neither." I wiped my eyes quickly, and we made our way back into the house where Wiz stood guard.

"You okay?" he asked, reaching out and massaging my shoulders.

As if it was a natural response, I wrapped my arms around his waist. I liked that he towered over me.

"Yes, I'm okay."

"You sure?"

"Mmhmm."

"I don't know where we go from here but know that you're safe with me. We've uncovered some shit about each other this past week, and I'm open to doing more of that to build on solid ground. And I know that shit that your ex pulled isn't something you're gonna heal from after three weeks. So long as you're willing to give me a fair chance, I wanna explore this. You good with that?"

I heard his words and smiled big. "Yeah, I'm good with that." We sealed the new journey with a kiss.

"And I'll still put a hole in that nigga at any given time. You just say the word."

"Oh, my God! Shut up, crazy."

"Let's eat, Beautiful." Slapping my butt, he grabbed my hand and led me into the dining room to join the rest of the crew.

How I managed to get rid of a dog ass nigga and lock down a gangsta in the matter of three weeks was a mystery to me, but my mama always said, "Good things come to the persistent," and Wiz was a persistent one.

IT'S 12:45. IT'S 95 DEGREES. I GOT A NEW NIGGA & MY NEW NIGGA GOT ME!

REVIEW

Did you enjoy the read?
Let us know how much by leaving us a review on Amazon
and Goodreads.

Snatched Up By A Hitta

Santa Sent Me A Real One For Christmas

Wet Dreams On Lockdown: The Unit Manager

Thug Me The Right Way

Thug Me The Right Way 2

Thug Me The Right Way 3

OTHER BOOKS BY

<u>URBAN AINT DEAD</u>

Tales 4rm Da Dale

The Hottest Summer Ever

Hittin' Licks For The Holidays: Atlanta

Wet Dreams On Lockdown: The Nurse

How To Publish A Book From Prison

By **Elijah R. Freeman**

Despite The Odds

By **Juhnell Morgan**

Good Girls Gone Rogue

Good Girls Gone Rouge 2

By **Manny Black**

Hittaz

Hittaz 2

Hittaz 3

Hittaz 4

Coldhearted

By **Lou Garden Price, Sr.**

This Time Won't You Save Me

This Time Won't You Save Me 2

By **Kyiris Ashley**

Stuck In The Trenches

Stuck In The Trenches 2

By **Huff Tha Great**

The Swipe

The Swipe 2

By **Toōla**

Melted the Heart of a Menace

Wet Dreams On Lockdown: Lieutenant Grace

By P. Wise

Merry Trapmas: Ice & Frost

By **Mia Sky**

Thug Me The Right Way

By **DiamondATL & Nai**

Atlantastan

By **Chris Green**

IN The Streetz

By **Tron Hill**

Wet Dreams on Lockdown: The Male C.O

By **Tamyra Griffin**

Wet Dreams On Lockdown: The Counselor

By **Paris Iman**

Wet Dreams On Lockdown: The Warden

By **Shawnice**

Wet Dreams On Lockdown: The Captain

By **TN Jones**

His Summer Side Piece
By **Kyiris Ashley**

Ridin' Forever
By **Telia Teanna**

Pretti & The Beast
By **P. Wise**

Atlantastan 2
By **Chris Green**

IN The Streetz 2
Tron Hill

BOOKS BY

URBAN AINT DEAD's C.E.O
<u>Elijah R. Freeman</u>

Triggadale

Triggadale 2

Triggadale 3

Tales 4rm Da Dale

The Hottest Summer Ever

Murda Was The Case

Murda Was The Case 2

Murda Was The Case 3

Hittin' Licks For The Holidays: Atlanta

Wet Dreams On Lockdown: The Nurse

How To Publish A Book From Prison

STAY CONNECTED

Follow
Elijah R. Freeman
On Social Media
FB: Elijah R. Freeman
IG: @the_future_of_urban_fiction